THE HEART OF LOVE

Book of Love, Book Nine

Meara Platt

ARE YOU SIGNED UP FOR DRAGONBLADE'S BLOG?

You'll get the latest news and information on exclusive giveaways, exclusive excerpts, coming releases, sales, free books, cover reveals and more.

Check out our complete list of authors, too!

No spam, no junk. That's a promise!

Sign Up Here

www.dragonbladepublishing.com

Dearest Reader;

Thank you for your support of a small press. At Dragonblade Publishing, we strive to bring you the highest quality Historical Romance from the some of the best authors in the business. Without your support, there is no 'us', so we sincerely hope you adore these stories and find some new favorite authors along the way.

Happy Reading!

CEO, Dragonblade Publishing

CHAPTER ONE

London, England
May 1821

WHATEVER HEATHER FARTHINGALE expected to see while in the garden at the break of dawn was not the big Scot, Robert MacLauren, tumbling over the high stone wall of Number One Chipping Way and dropping like a giant boulder onto the decorative wooden bench that stood against the garden wall. "Robbie!"

He did not tumble so much as crash down and land flat on his back atop the bench that was never going to support the muscled heft of him hitting it with such impact. Heather was not surprised when the bench began to sway precariously or when the wooden slats gave an ominous groan and sharply cracked.

She winced as the entire bench collapsed beneath his magnificent body, leaving him sprawled and dazed in all his golden glory.

Well, there was no point denying that Robert MacLauren, captain in the Scots Greys, the Crown's most distinguished cavalry regiment, was splendid in every way.

"Bollocks," he muttered, his words slurred as he gazed up at the early dawn sky. "Who moved the bloody wall?"

Well, perhaps this was not his finest moment.

"Robbie, are you hurt?" Heather hurried over to him and knelt by his side, ignoring the dampness of the grass now seeping through her thin robe and nightrail. The sun had barely peeked above the horizon, and she doubted any of the servants were stirring yet.

She'd only come outside to calm her betrothal jitters, especially since tonight was the night of the Marquess of Tilbury's grand ball, and she would be standing by his side now that they were soon to be married.

But here she was, unable to sleep while her stomach was in a tight coil, and never thought to encounter anything but the light breeze against her cheeks and the soft twitter of birds in the blossoming trees.

She had not expected the morning serenity to be shattered by this big Scot hurling himself over the wall from the fashionable Mayfair street known as Chipping Way and crashing onto the charming bench designed for sitting.

He'd smashed it to bits with his less than elegant dive.

"Are you drunk?" He did not need to answer. She smelled the ale on his breath and the acrid scent of cheap perfume on his jacket. "Ugh, you reek."

He lay atop the soft grass, blinking his eyes as he tried to focus on her. "Pixie? Is that you?"

"Yes, it's me. I ought to be furious with you." But she was afraid he had truly been injured. Getting him tended before he did more damage to himself was more important than lecturing him on the evils of his rakehell life.

She wasn't even certain he qualified as a true rakehell because he was too hardworking, had a well-defined code of honor, and had always been a complete gentleman in all his dealings with her. "What are you doing here at this hour?"

"Looking for ye, lass. And I've found ye. How's yer ankle?"

"Completely healed. Thank you for asking."

He smiled at her with enough warmth to melt a frozen sea. But this was Robbie's way, wasn't it? He knew how to turn on the charm whenever he wished.

Perhaps she was being too hard on him.

THE HEART OF LOVE

He had never attempted to take advantage of her. Quite the opposite, he'd appointed himself her protector and been quite wonderful to her until the Marquess of Tilbury had come along and taken up the role.

She shook out of her thoughts and touched him cautiously, afraid he might have broken a bone or cracked his head. "Oh, dear. The wood sliced your arm as it broke apart. You're bleeding. Please don't move. Let me get help."

He caught her hand in his rough palm, his touch surprisingly gentle. "No, lass. Give me a moment, and I'll manage on my own."

"Don't be stubborn. You need help. You fell off the wall."

"I could have fallen off the roof and not hurt myself. When ye're that drunk, yer body does no' feel it."

"You must be jesting. If you ever dare climb on the roof, I'll grab a loaded rifle and shoot you off it myself."

"I'll keep that in mind," he said with a warm smile that brought out the handsomeness of his features. "Just get me to the kitchen. I'll tend to the cut on my own. What are ye doing out here at this unholy hour? Isn't Tilbury's ball tonight? As his betrothed, ye'll be standing by his side. Ye want to make him proud, don't ye?"

"Yes…I just…" She frowned at him. "You had better sober up before the party. I won't have you showing up in your condition."

He reached up and caressed her cheek. "Heather," he said, pronouncing it *Heether* in his thick brogue, "I canno' go, lass."

"Why, Robbie? Are you still angry with me?" She wanted to cry, for his presence mattered to her more than she would ever dare admit.

He did not appear quite so drunk as he gazed at her with gorgeous eyes the green of a lush, Highlands glen. She had expected to find them reddened and dissipated, but they were surprisingly alert and clear. This was Robbie, somehow always looking splendid even when he ought to look like something the cat dragged through a fetid alleyway.

Even now, despite the gray light of dawn, a lone sliver of sunlight managed to shine down on his head so that his beautiful mane, cropped short at the sides and thick on top in military fashion, appeared golden.

This was one of his most irritating qualities, his ability to look as glorious as a Scottish sun god no matter what befell him.

He caressed her cheek again. "I could never be angry with ye. Why would ye think such a thing?"

"Because you left town so suddenly after the new year, and we never got to read that book together. You also stormed off after rescuing me the other day at Dahlia and Ronan's house. Now my sisters are worried because they think I've put a hex on myself by not reading the book with you, as I promised I would."

He closed his eyes and moaned. "Och, *The Book of Love*. I have it in my pouch. That's why I came here. I meant to return it to ye."

She glanced around. "I don't see your pouch."

"*Bollocks*. It's on the other side of the wall."

She rolled her eyes. "The one you almost broke your neck climbing over?"

He sat up slowly. "Aye, that one. My friends were supposed to toss it to me."

"Some friends," she muttered. "Were they the ones who heaved you over? You might have broken your neck." She suddenly gasped and scrambled to her feet. "What have they done with the book? Do you think they took it? They can't! I need it back."

She had no sooner said the words than an object came flying at her head and struck her cheek. She reeled and would have fallen had Robbie not caught her in his arms. "Pixie, are ye hurt?"

He sounded quite shaken and did not appear at all drunk now.

She was surprised by how quickly the pouch smacking her in the face had sobered him up. He'd shot to his feet with such speed, she realized he could not have broken any bones, or else he would never

4

have been able to move so fast.

Thank goodness for small mercies.

He held her in his arms and was now stroking her hair, possibly to calm himself as much as it was to calm her. Her hair was in a loose braid down her back and probably unkempt since she hadn't bothered to brush it before coming down here this morning.

She hadn't expected to encounter anyone.

"I'll be all right in a moment." But she had to rest her head against his chest when she suddenly felt lightheaded.

Her heart was still racing from the shock of being hit, but as she was now pressed to his chest, she could hear the rapid pounding of his heart and knew he had been rattled as well. "I'll kill them if they put a mark on ye."

She eased back and touched her cheek to the spot that was now throbbing. It also burned lightly and felt moist. She suddenly realized why. "Robbie, am I bleeding?"

The blaze of fire in his eyes and the gentle sweep of his thumb across her cheek was all the answer she needed.

"Tilbury's grand ball!" She would now be facing her guests—and worse, her betrothed—with a bruised cheek. What if it was swollen, too? How was she to appear elegant when she looked as though she'd been caught in a street brawl?

"We'll fix it, *Heether*. Ye'll look like a beautiful pixie, as ye always do." He glanced at the pouch that had landed at their feet, the straps now loosened, causing it to fall open to reveal the book's red leather binding peeking out.

He bent to retrieve the pouch and then surprised her by also lifting her in his arms. "What are you doing? I can walk. You're the one who needs carrying."

He laughed softly, a deep, glorious rumble. "Och, lass. I'd topple on ye and squash ye like a bug if ye ever tried to lift me."

"But Robbie, you fell, and now your arm is bleeding."

"I've suffered worse. Ye're the one my pawky friends hurt. Is yer head still spinning?"

She nodded. "How did you know?"

"I can see it in yer eyes."

She wrapped her arms around his neck because she was indeed feeling a little woozy. Or was it giddy? She could lie to herself and blame it on the pouch hitting her face. Or she could admit the truth she'd always dreaded. There was something about this big Scot that always made her head spin.

And now he was back after being away for months.

She squeezed her arms tightly around him and hoped he would not mistake it for a hug. Perhaps it was a hug.

She was glad to have him back.

She'd missed him.

"My little pixie," he whispered, kissing the top of her head. "I missed ye, too."

She wanted to cry.

Why did he have to come back today of all days? She was about to make her first formal appearance beside her betrothed. She and the Marquess of Tilbury would soon be married, and she would be a marchioness.

This was her dream.

This had always been her heart's desire. Ever since she was a little girl, she had always said she would grow up and marry a marquess, be a fine lady, and live in a fine house.

But Robbie had returned, bringing with him *The Book of Love*.

Was he about to shatter her childhood dreams?

CHAPTER TWO

ROBERT MACLAUREN DID not want to be back in London. He did not want to be holding Heather Farthingale in his arms…well, he did…but that was the problem. The innocent touch of his lips to her brow had wreaked silent havoc with his heart.

He had missed his little pixie desperately, and now that he was back, he did not know if he had the strength to let her go.

But he would have to, no matter how badly it broke his heart.

They were so wrong for each other.

Bollocks. Listen to him, talking to himself as though he had some claim on her when she was already betrothed and would soon marry.

And yet, was it a coincidence that having returned a mere week ago, he'd seen Heather twice and managed to have her in his arms each time? The first was when he'd caught her running out of her sister's house in tears only a few days ago. She'd been overset and not watching where she was going. He'd hauled her to safety after she'd almost run straight into a swiftly moving carriage.

Fortunately, she'd suffered nothing more than a lightly sprained ankle that was now healed, and just in time for her to open the dance with her betrothed, the Marquess of Tilbury, at his grand ball.

"I slipped out through the kitchen," Heather said, nestling her head on his shoulder as though it was the most natural thing to do, as though she belonged in his embrace. "We should return that way. All the other doors will still be locked."

"All right, lass." Her soft breath tickled his throat, and her rosebud lips were so close, he had only to dip his head to capture them in the proper kiss he ached to give her.

It would never happen.

She was betrothed to another.

He was happy for her. Indeed, she was a wonderful girl and deserved no less.

But less is what he was, for what could he offer her? The life of a Scottish captain's wife? To be taken away from all her loved ones to live in the Highlands, for that is where his home was, in Caithness. It may as well have been in the mountains on the moon for all the chance she'd ever have of seeing her sisters and the rest of her beloved family again.

He couldn't even hate the man she would soon marry, for the Marquess of Tilbury was a decent fellow and would treat Heather well. She deserved to be a fine lady. She would be an asset to him and a welcome addition to the *ton*, for she had a good, sweet heart and would use her position to help those less fortunate.

What could she do up in Caithness?

Not even *he* had a place there. His elder brother, Malcolm, was heir to the Earl of Caithness. He was merely fourth in line now that Malcolm had sons.

"Heather, why are there no servants stirring yet?" He was surprised to find they had the kitchen all to themselves. Shouldn't someone be up and about by now? Perhaps one of the scullery maids would come in soon to light the fire.

The house belonged to Romulus Brayden and Heather's cousin, Violet. The couple had married last year. Since Romulus was a captain in the Royal Navy and often away on assignment in Cornwall, he knew Heather was staying here to keep her cousin company.

"No, the staff starts later because Violet's been sleeping in lately."

He regarded her with concern. "Is she ill?"

Heather grinned. "She's about to give birth to a little Brayden. Although I don't think *little* can describe any of those Braydens, even the ones who are merely a day old. Romulus will be home within the next few days. Violet, out of sheer stubbornness, is not going to let that baby come before he returns."

Robbie cast her a genuine smile. "That's lovely, lass. Convey my congratulations to yer cousin."

"I will. But first, let's take care of you."

"No, lass. You first." A little more daylight shone into the kitchen as Robbie carried her in and carefully set her on a stool beside the door. He crossed to a cupboard and took out a cloth, then pumped water onto it, wringing it out before he returned to her side.

He knelt beside her and cupped her chin in his hand, hoping his touch was gentle. His hands were big and calloused, and she had such a soft, sweet face. He loved her big eyes and the way her little ears folded over at the top and stuck out just the littlest bit.

She was his pixie, small and graceful.

She put magic in his heart whenever they were together. "Ye have a slight cut along yer cheek. It bled a little. Ye ought to be good as new by the end of the week."

"End of the week?" She stared up at him in dismay as he dabbed the cloth against her cheek to wipe away the blood. "Robbie, how can I go to my own party looking as though I've been punched in the face? What will Tilbury think?"

"Ye'll put a little powder on it, and no one will notice."

"Powder? I don't have any."

He sighed. "I'm sure one of the older ladies in yer family will have some. And dinna worry about yer marquess. If he loves ye, he'll be relieved ye aren't more seriously hurt, and he'll think ye look beautiful anyway."

He finished dabbing at her cut and handed the damp cloth to her. "Here, hold it to yer cheek. I'll be right back."

Her eyes widened in surprise. "You're leaving me?"

"No, lass. I'm going to Romulus's study to fetch a bottle of brandy."

She leaped to her feet. "Haven't you had enough to drink? Didn't that graceless dive off the wall teach you anything?"

"When did ye turn into a lecturing shrew?" He frowned at her. "I dinna want to drink it. I need it to cleanse yer wound. Then I'll use it on my arm."

"Oh. Robbie, I'm so sorry." She obviously felt awful about insulting him. This was another thing he liked about her. She was softhearted, sometimes too much so. But he liked that about her, too.

"I'll be right back."

"No, wait. You're the one seriously hurt. I'll get the bottle. Sit down and remove your jacket and shirt. I want to see if you'll require stitches. If you do, I'll ask one of the footmen to fetch Uncle George."

"I'll be fine. I dinna need stitching." He let her think he was merely being stubborn, but he was worried, not knowing what might happen if she touched his bare skin. He'd always behaved himself around her, but she tempted him sorely, and he was not at his best just now.

One slip.

One mistake.

"Remove your jacket and shirt," she insisted, "or I'll grab the sharpest kitchen knife I can find and slice them off you."

"Och, first a shrew and now a bloodthirsty one at that. Not that I mind. I never cared for meek, simpering damsels. Verra well, be quick about it. There'll be hell to pay if ye're found in here alone with me. I may even have to marry ye. Yer marquess won't be happy about that."

"We both know that isn't going to happen." She rolled her eyes. "Stop jesting. Take off your shirt."

"No, lass. Not while ye're with me. I'm serious. Ye canno' be caught here when I remove it."

"What do you think I'll do? Fall into a swoon at your feet?" She hurried out of the kitchen and into the study to hunt for the brandy, easily finding it, for she was soon back with two bottles in hand. "Here it is, Robbie. But there was very little left in the bottle, so I also grabbed this unopened bottle of port wine."

He laughed when she handed the wine to him. "It's a little early to drink this. And it won't do much to help with a wound."

"It won't?" She pursed her lips, obviously dismayed. "I wasn't sure there would be enough brandy."

He set the wine on the window ledge and took the brandy. "It'll do, lass."

She studied him pensively. "Why is your shirt still on?"

"I told ye why. Do ye want to be a marchioness or not? Tilbury might overlook that we were caught in the kitchen together, but not if I've shed my clothes. Here's what I'll do, I'll tear off the sleeve. How's that? The shirt is ruined anyway." He set the brandy bottle aside and proceeded to rip away the fabric. He then took back the bottle and poured the brandy onto the cloth.

He pressed it to his ugly gash.

Tears welled in Heather's eyes as he began to cleanse it. "It's bad, Robbie. I think you will need those stitches, after all. Here, you missed some of the blood. Let me do it."

Why did the girl have to be so tenderhearted?

But he made no protest when she took the cloth from him.

Merciful heavens. Her fingers felt splendid as she lightly stroked his arm.

Once she'd wiped away the blood, she pressed the brandy-soaked cloth to the gash again and looked about for something to bind it. "The belt of my robe will have to do."

"Pixie, no. Are there no strips of cloth to be found here? Something we can rip up to properly bind this makeshift bandage to my arm?"

"I don't think so. Give me a moment to look." She searched through the cupboards and in the pantry before returning to Robbie's side. "I couldn't find anything suitable. Violet's linens are too fine, and they're matched sets. I can't break them up. Here, just use my belt."

"Och, no. It is a terrible idea."

She ignored his protests and cast him a warning scowl as she slipped it off her waist and began to wrap it around his arm. "See, it will be perfect."

Aye, perfect if she meant to put him in fiery torment.

Heat shot through him as her robe fell open to reveal the soft curves of her body and the perky fullness of her breasts beneath her nightrail.

Blessed saints.

In the next moment, he was tugging at her robe, drawing it closed. Of course, it wasn't going to remain that way with no belt to tie it, so he gave it another tug to primly close it and then held it securely in his fist.

She paused in the middle of binding the belt around his arm. "What are you doing?"

"Get on with it," he said, sounding quite surly. "And dinna bend over me like that."

"Who appointed you my grandmother? And *dinna* stare at me if I displease you so much. I'll be done in a moment. Stop scowling at me. I'm only trying to help."

"I can do the rest myself."

She was now poking the muscles of his upper arm, which were hard and tense because he was taut as a bowstring and about to snap. Only she was too innocent to realize it. But he understood what he was feeling. He'd read all about the attraction of the five senses. Sight. Touch. Taste. Scent. Hearing.

She stood too close, and he caught the scent of lavender on her skin.

It reminded him of the beautiful Scottish hills at the turn of the season, the hillsides lined in hues of purple and their soft, floral fragrance filling the air.

This was the scent of heaven.

Her smile was the light of heaven shining on a Highlands glen.

"Robbie…" She poked his arm again, interrupting his thoughts with her lilting voice. "Tending to you is like tending to an oak tree. Is the rest of your body this hard?"

He groaned.

She had no idea.

"I cannot imagine being an enemy soldier on the battlefield and seeing a man the size and power of you coming at me. I would have dropped my weapons and run."

"I would have protected ye on that battlefield. Ye know I'd never hurt ye."

"I know. There, all done," she said, admiring her handiwork.

He rose from the stool, took her by the shoulders, and nudged her into the seat he'd just vacated. "Your turn, lass. Keep the damn robe closed. I want to cleanse that little cut on yer cheek. Ye'll feel a sting, but it should no' hurt ye much."

He took her chin in the palm of his hand and tipped her head slightly to the side.

She flinched when he applied the brandy. "Ow!"

"Almost done. Be brave a moment longer."

She laughed. "I don't think I've been brave at all."

"Ye've been fine, lass," he said with a chuckle. "There." He set aside the cloth and then crossed to the table where he'd placed his pouch. He removed *The Book of Love* and held it out to her. "Here, it's yours to have now. Read it, Heather. Ye'll be glad ye did."

She stared at its faded leather binding, once a vivid red, but looking quite worn now. "I have to read it with you. I promised my sisters."

"No. I canno'. I won't be staying in London." He fought off the feeling of emptiness surging through him.

Her big eyes widened in dismay. "But you have to, Robbie. You need to read it with me, or we'll both be cursed for the rest of our lives. Please, set aside some time for me before you go."

"Pixie, ye canno' believe in such nonsense. Besides, your marquess won't like it."

"He doesn't have to know." But she blushed as she spoke the words, for she had to realize this was not the right way to embark on her life with Tilbury. There should never be lies between her and her betrothed. "I'll tell him, Robbie. I will."

"When?"

"I don't know. When it feels right. It's a delicate topic, not one that I can bring up in casual conversation. What am I to say? By the way, dear Tilbury. Funny thing. *Ha, ha.* You'll never guess what I've been doing. It really is quite humorous. I'm testing out love recipes with one of London's most handsome bachelors. Oh, and he happens to be an infamous womanizer."

"My reputation is exaggerated." He had been a hound in his younger days, he wasn't going to deny it. Nor would he deny that he'd maintained his casual ways until he'd met Heather.

Everything had changed for him the moment he'd set eyes on her. *The Book of Love* said that a man's low brain made him look at a woman's body first.

It hadn't been that way for him.

What he felt for Heather had never been merely physical.

Of course, he would not deny there was such an attraction.

Indeed, an achingly strong one.

But he had first been drawn to Heather by her smile and her big, sparkling eyes. He'd noticed the jaunty arch to her eyebrows and the impudent twist of her beautiful lips. He had itched to run his fingers through her lush brown hair. In truth, her hair was an exceptionally beautiful golden brown and perfectly framed her heart-shaped face and vivid, ocean blue eyes.

He'd fallen irrevocably in love with her the moment she'd tucked a stray curl behind her ear. Those little ears that stuck out like pixie ears.

He loved her face and the magic he felt whenever looking at her.

That her body was a thing of beauty did not hurt either.

But she was about to marry her marquess.

He was not going to interfere with her happiness.

"Robbie, are you worried that we'll fall in love if we read the book together?"

"No, my little pixie." It was already too late for him. All he could do now was take excruciating care never to reveal the raw, unguarded desire he felt for her.

Tears formed in her eyes. "Please come to Tilbury's ball. Do this for me, and I won't trouble you again."

"Och, dinna require it of me. Why should it matter to ye whether I'm there or not? Ye'll be too busy to notice me. Besides, I have other responsibilities." He stared at her, knowing just how to level that cold, dispassionate look.

"Aren't I a responsibility, too? You promised my sisters you would read the book with me. I wasn't the only one who made that promise. Isn't this why you came back? It has to be. You're too honorable ever to break your vow. It won't take us long to get through it. You've had it for months and must have read it several times over already. All you have to do is go over the important parts with me. Just once. How long will it take us? One afternoon?"

"It isn't the reading that worries me."

"Then what is it, Robbie?"

"It's—"

Heather never got her answer because an ear-piercing scream had both of them running out of the kitchen and toward the sound. "Violet!"

Dear heaven! Why had she screamed?

15

CHAPTER THREE

EATHER SAW HER cousin doubled over at the top of the stairs, her gown soaked. "My water broke," Violet said in tears. "It's too soon. Romulus won't be here for another three days."

Robbie picked her up gently. "Babes hold to their own schedule, Violet. Let nature take its course. Heather, where's her bedchamber?"

"This way." She hurriedly led him down the hall to the master quarters. She checked the sheets to see if they were wet since Violet had said her water broke. Fortunately, the bed was dry. She must have gotten up, sensing something was happening, and then the water soaked through her nightgown and onto the carpet. "Wait, Robbie. Don't put her back in bed yet. Let me change her into a dry nightgown."

She ran to Violet's wardrobe and grabbed one. "Violet, can you stand up on your own?"

She nodded. "I think so."

Violet was still crying as Robbie set her on her feet with exquisite care. "Heather will stay with ye. I'll run next door now and fetch yer aunt."

She caught hold of his hand, suddenly forgetting her tears and her contractions. Her gaze shot from one to the other, and she appeared utterly confused. "Robbie, why are you here?"

He gave a mirthless laugh. "It's a long story. Heather will tell ye. Let me fetch yer aunt for ye."

Heather was never more glad to have family living next door.

Most of the houses on Chipping Way were inhabited by members of the Farthingale family. Violet and her husband resided at Number One. Heather's aunt and uncle, Sophie and John Farthingale, resided at Number Three. They were also aunt and uncle to Violet. Lady Eloise Dayne resided at Number Five. Eloise wasn't a blood Farthingale, but her two grandsons were married to Sophie and John's daughters, Daisy and Laurel, and this was close enough to make her a member of the family.

Heather nodded to him. "Hurry back, Robbie."

"Aye, lass." He took off without delay, shutting the door behind him to lend them privacy, and obviously eager to be away. No doubt, he regretted ever stopping by when he could have simply sent a messenger to deliver the book to her.

Why he'd come by at the crack of dawn baffled her. But she supposed he'd meant to drop it off last night before he went carousing, forgot about it, and now being stupidly drunk, thought it would be appropriate to drop it off on his way home after a night out.

Violet gasped, overcome by another contraction.

Heather's thoughts immediately returned to her. "Aunt Sophie will be here soon. Let me make you comfortable in the meantime." She removed Violet's soaked nightgown and quickly grabbed a clean washing cloth and soap she found next to a basin and ewer perched on her bureau. After dipping the cloth in water, she rubbed a little of the soap on it, and then returned to Violet to gently wash her down.

If only the rest of the birthing would be so easy. She had no experience delivering a child. How would she, when her parents had done their utmost to keep their girls ignorant of all matters of this nature?

She was the youngest of three sisters and used to being spoiled and pampered. She did not have Holly's quiet elegance or Dahlia's wit and grace. Holly was her eldest sister, and Dahlia was the middle child.

As for her, she was their parents' unintended mistake. And yet, they had always been certain she would be the one to marry a nobleman and become one of the *ton's* leading ladies. They'd pushed all three of their daughters to marry into the Upper Crust, and she was the one they would have placed their wagers on to accomplish it.

Perhaps it was because she'd proclaimed she was going to be a marchioness at the ripe old age of five and had stuck to this belief throughout her life.

Now, it was about to come true.

But what mattered most at the moment was making Violet comfortable. She dried her off and then helped her on with a fresh nightgown. "Let me get you into bed."

She drew aside the covers as her cousin, looking beautiful even though she was the size of a bull walrus, climbed in.

But Violet was no sooner settled than she began to ask questions. "Are you going to tell me what Robert MacLauren was doing here at this hour of the morning? And why is his sleeve torn and your belt wrapped around his arm?"

"It's innocent," Heather said, plumping Violet's pillows so that she was propped up comfortably.

"These explanations always are." She grinned despite her contractions. "Tell me before the others arrive."

"I happened to be standing in the garden, when..." She quickly related all that had happened.

Violet smiled. "That is so romantic."

"What? No, it isn't in the least. He was merely returning the book to me."

Violet rolled her eyes. "And you think this is just coincidence? Tilbury's ball is tonight."

Heather nibbled her lip. "I'll have to miss it. So will Aunt Sophie. She cannot leave your side, and neither will I."

"Don't be ridiculous. I'll have the finest midwife in London with me within the hour as well as Uncle George, who will remain close by in the event he is needed. I will kick both you and Aunt Sophie out of here as soon as they arrive. You need to look beautiful for your special night."

Heather took a gentle hold of her cousin's hand. "It isn't important. Don't you want me to stay with you?"

"Absolutely not. You are to rest and pamper yourself. The ball is what you need to pay attention to. I'll be right here once it's over. And I'm sure you and every other Farthingale and Brayden in London will stop in after the ball to find out if the babe has popped out yet. More will come traipsing through here tomorrow. I think I must engage a secretary to fend you all off."

Heather laughed. "Will you let me sit by your side once I'm back from Tilbury's ball? You know I won't be able to sleep until I see your new son or daughter and know you are all right."

"Yes, I'd love your company then."

"I think I hear the servants stirring downstairs. I ought to let them know what is happening."

Violet kept hold of her hand. "No, Heather. Stay with me until Aunt Sophie arrives."

"Of course." She stifled her tears, realizing that despite Violet's excitement, she was scared. No wonder she was overset that Romulus was not with her. Even though he would not be permitted in their bedchamber, just knowing he was close by would have heartened her.

Violet gasped as another contraction overwhelmed her. "Finish telling me what is going on between you and Robbie."

"Nothing is going on. I'm going to marry Tilbury. But Robbie and I must read that book together. My sisters made us promise. He doesn't want to. Not that I blame him. I was the one who refused at first."

"So, he took the book and went away."

Heather nodded. "Now he's back."

"For a significant reason, Heather. What does your heart tell you to do?"

She squeezed her cousin's hand. "My life is here. My heart's desire has always been to marry a marquess. Besides, you know Robbie's reputation with the ladies. How can I ever trust him to be faithful?"

The notion appeared to surprise Violet. "Oh, Heather. You are so wrong about him. That big Scot will honor and love you until the day he dies."

"How can you say that?" She shook her head. "He came over the wall drunk and reeking of stale perfume. But let's not speak of him now. I hear more voices in the hall. Aunt Sophie's on her way up."

"Then I had better say this quickly. Romulus and I read the book together. It showed us how to open our hearts and see the truth. Don't fight it, Heather. Let it guide you to your true happiness. If your life is meant to be with Tilbury, then you will know it without a doubt."

"And if it isn't?"

"Are you worried it will lead you to Robbie?" Violet arched an eyebrow. "He's worried about it as well."

"He doesn't want to attend Tilbury's ball."

Violet nodded. "Can you blame him? His heart must be breaking."

"Oh, I doubt it. Then why doesn't he say something to me? Why run away? Violet, you are deeply in love with your husband, so you think all men must be as honorable and wonderful as him. I'm not saying Robbie is a bad person. He isn't at all. But he has a roving eye. We all know it. He may intend to reform, but for how long? Women are constantly making advances to him. Beautiful, elegant ladies, too. I've seen it myself."

They said no more as Aunt Sophie arrived and sat on the other side of the bed to get a closer look at Violet. "How long between contractions, my dear?"

She and Violet stared at each other. They had been so busy chatting, neither of them had thought to time her pains. Heather did not realize it was something they ought to have been doing.

Sophie shook her head and laughed softly. "It doesn't matter. We'll start as of now."

"What should I do, Aunt Sophie?" Heather rose, wanting to be helpful but having no idea how to go about it.

"Let the staff know what is going on. Have Violet's cook prepare light refreshments since we'll have people stopping in throughout the day. You'll have to serve as hostess. Well, sort of as liaison between the family and us as they gather downstairs. Can you do this, Heather?"

"Of course."

"Well, I know you can. But what I meant is, Tilbury's ball is this evening. You ought to be well rested and looking beautiful for it." She shook her head and sighed. "We'll have to hide that little cut to your cheek. Captain MacLauren mentioned it when he spoke to me and John."

Heather's hand went to her cheek.

She'd forgotten about it in all the excitement.

Sophie was now staring at her.

Heather groaned. "Violet will tell you why he was here. And injured. And why my belt is on his arm. It really is quite innocent."

She rolled her eyes. "I've been through it with my daughters. Yes, these explanations always are."

Heather gave her aunt a kiss on the cheek and her cousin a light kiss on the forehead before running downstairs to the kitchen to inform the staff of what was happening. The housekeeper happened to be the niece of Aunt Sophie's long-time cook. "Miss Mayhew, we'll need to prepare for company throughout the day."

The young woman smiled. "I used to be in service at your aunt and uncle's house next door. This will be simple."

Heather laughed. "Then I know you'll have it all well in hand. Thank you." She saw the book Robbie had come here to return to her sitting on the table. She picked it up and glanced around for his pouch and jacket. There was no sign of them.

Her heart gave a little tug.

"Miss Heather," the housekeeper said quietly. "I think he's still in the study with your Uncle John."

She blushed. "Thank you, Miss Mayhew."

She hurried to the study with the book in hand, taking care to keep her robe closed because her uncle was probably apoplectic already. He had to be wondering what Robbie was doing here at this early hour.

The study door was shut, so she knocked lightly and then barged in without awaiting permission to enter. Robbie was casually leaning against the desk, his arms crossed over his massive chest, while her uncle was seated in one of the comfortable chairs beside it. To her relief, they appeared quite calm.

She gave her robe another tuck to hold it securely closed—a gesture noticed by Robbie, for he arched an eyebrow and tossed her a tender smile.

The loveliness of his smile sent her reeling.

The events of the morning suddenly crashed down on her like a giant wave. In the next moment, she was crying like a ninny. More giant waves of feeling crashed down on her, and she did not know how to hold them back.

Suddenly, Robbie wasn't smiling any more. "Heather, all is well. Why are ye crying, lass?"

It was the worst question he could have asked because at this moment, she knew the reason why. Yes, she was overset because she had a cut to her cheek. Yes, she was worried about Violet giving birth. But the reason she was crying...*dear heaven*. She thought Robbie had gone away, and she was never going to see him again.

She must have spoken the words aloud because her Uncle John was staring up at the ceiling and muttering "Why, Lord?" and Robbie was looking at her as though he'd just been fatally shot.

Perhaps walking in here had not been a good idea.

Robbie took the book out of her hands and set it aside. "Sit down, Heather." He tried to guide her to the chair beside her uncle. At first, she resisted, but then she sank down in it and buried her face in her hands.

No one spoke for the longest time.

Robbie was kneeling beside her and stroking her hair. Finally, he groaned. "I'll come by tomorrow. We're going to read that book together as we promised yer sisters. Then ye will understand what true love is all about and marry yer marquess."

She looked up at him through a cloud of tears. "Will you come to the ball tonight?"

"Oh, for pity's sake," her uncle muttered. "I'll not have a fight break out over you at Tilbury's ball."

Robbie immediately spoke up. "There'll be no fight, Mr. Farthingale. For my part, I'll not throw a fist at Tilbury." He turned back to Heather. "No, I will not be there. It is safest for ye if I stay away. It isn't me I'm worried about doing something foolish. It's you, lass."

"What do you think I'll do?"

He gave her cheek a light caress. "I have no idea. That's what scares me most."

Her uncle cleared his throat. "Here's what you are both going to do this very morning. Go your separate ways and get properly washed and dressed. Captain MacLauren, you are going to return here immediately after making yourself presentable. I don't care if you have scheduled an audience with the king. Reschedule it. You are to present yourself here."

Heather stared at him, confused. "Why, Uncle John?"

He glared at the book. "I don't know what nonsense that book contains. Perhaps it isn't nonsense since six of my nieces have managed to make love matches after toting it around. So, you are going to do the same, Heather. Not with Tilbury, since you haven't once brought up his name amid your flurry of tears. You are going to read it with Captain MacLauren. This morning. This afternoon. However long it takes you to get through it *before* the ball. You will not put this off until tomorrow."

Robbie ran his hand roughly through his hair. "Bollocks."

"You will sit outside in plain sight of us all and—"

"We can't sit. Robbie broke the bench when he fell over the wall."

Her uncle showed no expression as he said, "Of course, he did. Why am I not surprised? Take a blanket and sit under a shade tree. Stand on your head if you prefer. Just read that book together. Heather, if you can still marry Tilbury after this, then I'm going to need the stiffest drink I've ever had in my life."

Robbie looked as though he wanted to smash every object in the study. "I'll return in an hour." He grabbed his pouch and stalked out without so much as a nod in her direction.

"Uncle John, I think this is a terrible idea. He's so angry."

"I don't care. What are you two playing at?"

Heather swallowed hard. "What do you mean?"

"I've never seen two people more afraid of reading that book."

"I'm the one who's afraid. Robbie's read it, probably several times over by now."

"So that's why he wanted to wait until tomorrow to read it with you. He thinks your standing beside the marquess, acting as his hostess at the ball, will somehow remove all possibility of your canceling the wedding? You'll be a marchioness as you've always wanted to be. By delaying until tomorrow, he thinks he's ensuring the outcome. Hah! He's deluding himself if he thinks the delay will work. But I have one question for you."

She nodded. "What is it, Uncle John?"

"Have you ever once considered Tilbury's feelings in all this?"

CHAPTER FOUR

ROBBIE'S GRANDUNCLE, THE Earl of Caithness, possessed a modest townhouse on the outskirts of Mayfair, maintained by a butler and housekeeper who were an elderly married couple in service to the earl since Robbie was an infant. He was residing there for now since the barracks housing the Scots Greys was closed while the regiment was up in Scotland.

"Good morning, Crawford," he said, striding in when the butler opened the door to him. "Kindly ask Mrs. Crawford to set out some bandages for me."

The man's eyes widened in alarm. "Are ye injured, Captain Mac-Lauren?"

"A little cut. Nothing serious. And I need to bathe." He took the stairs two at a time up the staircase and marched down the hall to his bedchamber. He tossed off his ruined jacket and shirt, only then realizing he still had Heather's belt strapped to his arm. Some of the blood from his gash had seeped through and stained it.

He sighed, knowing he could not return it to Heather in this condition. He'd ask Mrs. Crawford to wash it. Perhaps she could boil the stain out. Otherwise, he'd purchase a new robe for the pixie.

He pulled off his boots, grabbed a fresh pair of trousers, and returned downstairs to help Crawford fill up the tub. The weather was warm enough that he did not need to put Mrs. Crawford to the trouble of heating water for his bath. He would clean up just as well in the cold as in hot. The loch waters in Caithness were almost frigid, and he and his brother often bathed in them until the first snow fell.

Once in the kitchen, he removed the belt and bloodied cloth to inspect the gash. *Bollocks.* It was worse than he'd thought. He would need stitches and a more thorough cleansing of the wound to keep his blood from getting infected. "Crawford, fetch me the bootleg whisky."

"At once, Captain MacLauren."

Mrs. Crawford eyed him sternly. "A lady's belt?"

"It isn't what you think. I was not undressing her." He poured a pail of water into the tub that was set out beside the hearth. A fire was lit for cooking but not needed for warmth. Still, he had been out all night, and his body was feeling sore, especially from that drunken dive he'd taken.

The heat from the fire would do him good.

"Then what were ye doing to the lass? Or were ye just watching her as she undressed?" She shook her head in disapproval. "Ye need to reform yer wicked ways, laddie. Ye need to find yerself a genteel lass and make a proper home for yerself."

He supposed the odor of cheap perfume on his jacket would lead anyone to the wrong conclusion. Aye, he had been in one of those gaming hells where more than mere gaming went on. Aye, he had been approached by more than one female...and rubbed up against more than once. But he had declined their invitations as he had all women since meeting Heather.

Which left him bloody, blazing frustrated for the obvious reasons, but especially because no one believed he had reformed or ever could reform.

Of course, he wasn't helping himself by frequenting these ill-reputed establishments, even if it was only to engage in a game of cards or share a drink with his companions. Obviously, he needed to cultivate a better class of companions.

The problem was, his two best friends, Joshua Brayden and his brother, Ronan, were now married to Heather's sisters and happily settled. These Brayden men returned home every evening to their loving wives.

He returned home to nothing.

He did not even have a home to call his own, returning every night either to the barracks when his regiment was in town or his granduncle's residence whenever they were not.

He shook out of the thought and finished pouring water into the tub. He set up the screen to provide himself a little privacy and then washed his hair and body. Once done, he wrapped the drying cloth around himself and opened the bottle of whisky. The fumes alone were enough to choke a horse.

The brandy he'd applied earlier to his arm packed a sting.

This home-brewed whisky was going to light a fire up his arse.

He doused a washing cloth with it and then slapped the wet cloth to his arm. His eyes turned watery as the burn shot up his arm and blazed through his body. He held it in place for several minutes, then had Mrs. Crawford bind the wound as best as she could. He knew George Farthingale would be at Violet's home by the time he returned there. He would ask the good doctor to put a few stitches in then.

He shaved, donned a clean uniform, and set off for Chipping Way once again.

By this time, the day had turned beautiful. The sun was shining, and a light breeze carried the scent of spring blooms. His horse needed a bit of exercise, so he saddled Gallant, one of the finest cavalry horses ever bred, and took him for a quick trot through the park before riding over to Violet's house.

The valiant steed had seen him through the Napoleonic Wars. His regiment had mostly served as back up forces for the main English army. But they had taken the lead in the Battle of Waterloo, and he owed his life to Gallant. They had worked as one during the course of battle, Gallant responding to his every subtle movement. A tap with his right knee. A tap with his left. An easing or tightening on his reins.

For every man in his cavalry regiment, their horse was more precious than gold. For many, their horse was more precious than a wife. "Gallant, are ye prepared to meet Heather? Ye'll have to tell me what ye think of her."

The beast snorted in response.

"But dinna make the mistake of falling in love with her. She isn't ours to keep."

He turned onto Chipping Way and rode up to the front gate. He was not surprised when Heather came running out of the house to greet him before he'd managed to dismount. Her hair was done up in a casual twist, taking on an extraordinarily beautiful, golden brown tone as the sun shone down upon those silken curls.

Her morning gown was the same azure color of her eyes. It was a modest affair and looked quite lovely on her. "Ye look pretty, lass."

She blushed but seemed quite pleased by the compliment. "Dahlia helped me choose the color. She has an eye for such things, doesn't she?"

"Indeed." He tried to contain his smile, but it was a hopeless endeavor. The lass was magic to his heart, and he could not hold back the upward twitch of his lips as he dismounted. "Are ye ready to do some reading, lass?"

She nodded, her eyes sparkling as she cast him a pixie smile. "Is this your gray?"

"Aye, he's mine."

She stroked the stallion's nose. "He's a beauty, Robbie. What's his name?"

"Gallant. I raised him from a foal." Why had he told her that? Why would she care? "Shall we get on with it?"

She arched an impudent eyebrow. "The dreaded reading?"

He hadn't been keen on discussing the book with her today. At this point, not ever. She'd be married to Tilbury by next week. He knew this was an act of cowardice on his part, but he didn't care. They were both afraid of what would be revealed to them.

Heather had her dream to marry a marquess. He had no dreams, only the stark reality of what he could offer her as a husband, which was embarrassingly little.

Simpler to leave things as they were.

She with her marquess.

He…with whatever his life would bring.

His feelings would have been different if Heather had come from a poor family with no connections to speak of. But she came from a large, loving family. She was connected to some of the finest noble houses in England through advantageous marriages among the Farthingales, and now she was about to be the next debutante in the family to marry into one of those noble houses.

She would spend her days entertaining in a fashionable home and living a prestigious life in London. All she had to do was exchange vows with Tilbury, and then all her dreams would come true.

"My cousin, Laurel, is one of the finest horse breeders in England," Heather said, breaking into his thoughts. "She is John and Sophie's daughter and married to Lady Dayne's grandson, Graelem."

"Aye, I've heard of her. She's well known in Scotland, too. Baroness Moray. She raises the finest horses, including the grays we purchase for our regiment."

"The *ton* is shocked by her, of course. Graelem is quite proud of her abilities. He is not ashamed to let everyone know he defers to her decisions in all matters concerning their stables."

"That's because he's a pragmatic Scot. We judge on merit, not on inane rules designed to shut others out."

She nodded in agreement. "Those rules are quite repugnant, aren't they? Laurel has to make special arrangements to view the bloodstock whenever there is an auction at Tattersalls. In public, the men who run these horse auctions pretend to be appalled by her, but they all privately come to her begging for advice. It's so unfair, and who are they fooling?"

He loved to hear her talk, for her voice held a musical quality. "We have more respect for women in Scotland. We dinna have these same restrictions in our societies or our daily life."

"My cousin Lily also enjoys living in Scotland. Her husband is Ewan Cameron, the Duke of Lotheil's grandson. She's active in several of Edinburgh's most distinguished academies. However, no matter her abilities, London's Royal Society will never admit her as one of their own. If not for Ewan's grandfather, she would not even be permitted to lecture there. He's chairman, and he's a crusty, old goat who loves to stick it to those stodgy blowhards on his board of directors."

He nodded. "She lectured there recently."

"Nearly causing a riot among the Fellows." Heather grinned. "Yes, she wrote a brilliant monograph on baboon colonies. She takes great delight in comparing the Fellows to her baboons. They'd run her out of London if they could, but they dare not while the duke remains as chairman and wields tremendous power over them. Unfortunately, he doesn't have the votes to change their rules and allow women to be admitted as members. But he does hold sway over who lectures there and takes glee in scoffing at these antiquated restrictions."

She paused a moment and pensively stroked Gallant's nose. "The duke used to be her biggest detractor, and now he's her staunchest ally. I suppose miracles can happen. Do you believe in miracles, Robbie?"

"No, lass."

She laughed lightly. "Also a pragmatic Scot, are you? And I was raised to be a little princess. Always pampered and indulged. It feels empty. But I think I can do good for those in need once I am a marchioness. I don't mind working hard. I would love to feel useful. I haven't even discussed this with Tilbury. Do you think he'd forbid my charitable work?"

"I dinna know. Why haven't ye asked him?"

She nibbled her lip, now fretting. "I should have, shouldn't I? There's so much we haven't discussed. I close up when I'm around him, Robbie. I don't know why. It isn't his fault. I think he'd listen. The problem is with me. I want to do something important, but I don't know where my strengths lie."

In the next moment, she rolled her eyes and cast him one of her magical, impish grins. "I do know my weaknesses, however. I am dreadful when it comes to science. Lily shall have no competition from me."

"You're a clever lass. I'm sure it was the instructor's fault for failing to make it interesting to you."

She shook her head and let out a sparkling laugh. "Oh, my poor tutor. I think my parents chose him purposely because he was a crushing bore, and they did not wish him to turn me into a bluestocking. After all, how was I to attract a marquess if I buried my nose in books?"

Too bad Heather had been discouraged from exploring her scientific mind. This might have been something he could have offered her and something to bind them. In Scotland, she would have been treated as an equal in all her research undertakings.

He handed the reins to Violet's groom and glanced toward the house. "Is yer Uncle George here yet?"

"Yes, he's in the study. He just looked in on Violet and assured us that all is proceeding in the ordinary course. But he'll stay close, and he's brought his medical bag, just in case."

"I need a moment with him. Why don't you fetch the book and wait for me in the garden?"

She pursed her lips as she studied him. "It's the gash, isn't it? You do need stitches. I knew it."

He groaned. "Pixie, just get the book and meet me outside. All right?"

"Are all Scots as thickheaded as you?" She left him to run upstairs.

He strode into the study, relieved to find George Farthingale in there alone. "Doctor, may I trouble ye a moment?"

"Come in, Captain MacLauren. What can I do for you?"

Robbie shut the door behind him and pointed to the injured spot. "I managed to slice my arm earlier this morning. I've doused it in whisky, but I think it requires a few stitches."

George nodded. "Have a seat. Let me have a look at you. It will give me something to do while I wait around for Violet to need me. Hopefully, the babe will come without a problem, and I'll be totally irrelevant. Take off your jacket and shirt. Let me see what you've done to yourself."

Robbie glanced at the door.

"No one will come in. Violet's butler is showing everyone into the parlor. They've set up refreshments for their visitors. John's in there now, acting as host. Sophie's still upstairs with Violet, but she'll be down soon to greet any visitors who come by."

He shed his jacket and shirt, then carefully removed the binding from his wound.

George's expression revealed nothing as he studied the gash. "You've done a good job of cleaning it. Nasty looking thing. How did it happen?"

"A piece of wood broke off and tore through my shirt and jacket, piercing my arm."

He arched an eyebrow as he felt along Robbie's arm. "Doesn't appear any of the splintered wood lodged in your skin. Good. Any connection to the shattered bench in Violet's garden?"

He gave a light groan. "Yes."

George sighed. "I shouldn't ask. I shouldn't want to know how it happened or why it happened. Since Violet is the size of a small whale at the moment and happily married to Romulus, I must assume this broken bench is somehow connected to Heather."

Robbie grimaced. "Do ye really wish for an answer?"

"No." He reached into his medical bag and removed the needle and sutures. "The whisky you've rubbed on it ought to keep the area numb while I work on you."

Robbie nodded. "I've been shot before and speared with a bayonet. I can manage a few stitches."

"You fought with the Scots Greys."

"Aye, but no serious battles until Waterloo. We primarily served as support for the English regiments. We were ambushed more than a few times in the course of the war, so the Greys were experienced going into this final battle." He pointed to his side, where there was a hardly noticeable scar. "A rifle shot grazed me here. The bayonet wound was more serious. Left a scar along my thigh. Bastard tried to slice my leg open. Fortunately, I managed to shoot him before he succeeded."

They continued to chat as George treated him. "I served as a doctor in the Peninsular War during those early years," George said, concentrating on his stitches.

"It must have been rough. I was too young to join then, but I wanted to. I tried to sneak away to enlist once when I was all of fifteen, but my granduncle, the Earl of Caithness, caught up to me in Aberdeen. He boxed my ears and threatened to toss me in the dungeon if I dared to run off before I turned sixteen."

George glanced up. "That's still too young."

"I know. But I did no' think so at the time. I wanted to join the fight."

They were too busy talking to hear the light knock on the door. Or had Heather even bothered to knock? The next thing Robbie knew, she was stepping into the room uninvited.

George looked up. "Heather, what are you doing in here? Shut that door!"

Instead of running out, she merely closed the door behind her and rushed to Robbie's side. "I knew it! How badly is he hurt, Uncle George?"

"*Heether*, get *oot*." Robbie gritted his teeth, his brogue on full display as he shouted at her. He was furious she'd come in here. Was she trying to get them caught in a compromising position? Did she think the presence of her uncle would save her from ruin?

It wouldn't.

She set her book aside and sat on the opposite side of him, taking his hand even though he did not want her touching him. "How long will this take?"

"I'm done," George said. "Twelve stitches in all. The problem is not with his arm. It will heal now that I've sewn it up. I'm going to apply a poultice to it and bind it again."

Heather wrinkled her nose. "Ugh. The same smelly unguent you gave Ronan when he was injured?"

George nodded. "Yes, the very same." He quickly applied it and rebound the bandage. "Get dressed, Captain MacLauren, before you draw more women in here."

Heather frowned. "It's only me, Uncle George."

He shook his head and gazed heavenward. "Only you? Heather, you do realize you are the worst person to be in here, don't you? Are you, or are you not about to marry your marquess?"

"She is," Robbie said at the same time she blurted, "I don't know."

Robbie's heart stopped in that instant. But he quickly regained his senses and ran a hand through his hair in consternation. "Blessed, bloody saints. Are ye serious, lass? This has been yer lifelong dream."

"Then why is everyone insisting we read the book together? No one trusts me to make the right decision. You all think I'm a child and don't know my own mind. You all think you know what I need better than I do."

Robbie gave her hand a little squeeze. "Ye're right. But that's what comes of having meddling families who wish ye to be happy. They're doing it out of love because they want you to make a true love match."

He rose, bringing her up with him. "Turn around while I put on my shirt."

She turned to face her uncle, watching him close up his medical bag. "Uncle George, why is everyone worried that I don't love Tilbury? He's a good man. A kind person. I like him very much. How is this terrible?"

He frowned at her. "How did you get that cut on your cheek? That bench?"

"No, a flying book. It hit me in the face. Robbie tended to it."

He grunted. "He did a good job. But that's what comes with learning more than a little medicine on the battlefield, right MacLauren?"

Robbie nodded as he finished tucking in his shirt and donning the jacket of his uniform. "A matter of necessity if one hoped to survive the war."

"Heather, borrow a little powder for it from Hortensia. That ought to hide the cut and bruising well enough."

"Thank you, Uncle George. I will." She turned to Robbie now that he was decent. "Let's get through this book before noontime."

They'd been up since before cock's crow, and although it felt as though half the day was gone, it was barely nine o'clock in the morning. After thanking her uncle again, he strode outside with Heather. She had spread the blanket under a shade tree. She placed the book atop the blanket while he settled with his back propped against the trunk of the tree.

Heather sat beside him.

"Did ye have a chance to read any of the chapters before I arrived?" He casually pillowed one hand behind his head and tilted his face toward the sun as it filtered through the leaves.

"I managed to read the first three chapters and then skimmed through the others. I was worried that you were going to defy my uncle's wishes and not come back."

"I told him I would. I keep to my word."

She placed a hand gently on his forearm. "I know you do, Robbie. I was only teasing you."

"Shall we start at the beginning?" he asked, still feeling the heat from her touch even after she'd slipped her hand away.

"And talk about the man's low brain and high brain? I think I understand the concept. But is it true, Robbie? Do men really have two brains?"

"Aye, lass. Although I'm more of a mind to call it two parts of the same brain. One part contains our youthful, immature yearnings and desires. It is the thoughtless brain that indulges our urges without regard for others. We see a pretty lass and want her. We think nothing of taking her and then going on our merry way."

"The book says this is the true nature of men. That you are not fashioned to be faithful to just one woman but are compelled to...mate with as many females as possible in order to produce offspring." She frowned but continued. "For this reason, you seek out healthy females. You regard us as you would your breeding stock."

Robbie sighed. "It is no' a pretty way to describe the way we men think. I suppose it could be said the marriage mart is not much different than an auction at Tattersalls. Young women are paraded before us so that we may select the one who is right for us. We fancy it up with balls and musicales and elegant supper parties. The ladies bedeck themselves in fine gowns and sparkling gems. But it is all for one purpose, to obtain a marriage proposal, and then get on about the business of breeding heirs."

"You make it sound awful, Robbie."

"I dinna mean to. It is the way of life for all creatures, perhaps with some variation, but always necessary for our survival. Women have their needs as well. Just as a male desires to sire offspring, the female requires her male to remain faithful in order to protect her and their offspring."

"Or else they'd be eaten by wolves. That's what it says in the book."

"Aye, lass. So, at some point, the man's brain must adapt to this rational need and remain faithful to the woman he's chosen to bear his sons and daughters. The ability to adapt to that rational need is the man's higher brain function."

She was looking at him as she spoke, hanging upon his every word as though gold spewed from his lips. He was merely explaining the thoughts of the author who wrote the book.

"Violet is a perfect example of this. Isn't she, Robbie? She is now having Romulus's child. She is at her most vulnerable."

"Aye, and no doubt Romulus is mad with worry and desperate to get back here in time to be by her side."

She cast him a wry smile. "Obviously, he has a well-defined higher brain. He wants to protect Violet with all his heart and soul."

"As any decent man would want to do with the woman he loves. As the book says, he canno' simply mate with her and then abandon her and their offspring. They are no' in danger from real wolves, of course. Those beasts represent any danger a woman at her most vulnerable would have to face. This is why Romulus has made certain Violet has a proper home, food, and shelter. He also knows his family and hers will protect her whenever he is not here to do it. But this is also why Violet chose him as her husband. He is the powerful male she knows will protect her and their children from harm."

"Is this why I am drawn to Tilbury?"

"It is one of the reasons. There ought to be more, but those are described in the next chapters."

She pinched her lips. "I want to know more about that low brain function, the one that compels a man to mate with healthy females. Does this describe you, Robbie? Is this how you look at all women? Is this how Tilbury looks at me?"

He did not particularly like the way she thought of him. Of course, he'd built up a reputation in his younger days that he was not proud of and could not seem to shed even though the worst of it was in the past. "I think Tilbury has a well-developed high brain function. He may have looked at your body at first glance and liked what he saw, but he quickly moved beyond it to choose you as his life mate. I canno' fault him for his judgment."

"Is this also what you noticed about me first?" She blushed. "The book says a man looks at a woman's...bosom first. Is this what you did?"

One of the things he'd learned in reading the book was the need for honesty. He could only ever tell Heather the truth, no matter how difficult it was to reveal. In this instance, it was not difficult at all. Indeed, it was a revelation to him because he'd never given it much thought until just now. "No, the first thing I noticed about ye was your smile and the starlight in your eyes. Only afterward did I bother to look lower."

"Is this what you usually do?"

"No, mostly I am exactly the sort of low-brain male this book describes. Eyes drawn to a woman's bosom. Then afterward, the rest of her body. Last, I look at her face. In my lowest moments, there were times I dinna even bother to look at the woman's face. But that's all in the past now."

She tucked her legs under her, all the while casting him a dubious look. "Truly?"

"Aye, truly."

She appeared to accept his response, although her lips were now puckered in thought. "Why was it different with me?"

He closed his eyes. "I dinna know. It just was. Because I knew right away ye were someone special. Lass, ye were never someone I would bed and then abandon. Ye were never someone I could forget."

"Do you think Tilbury feels the same way?"

He turned to glance at Heather. Who would not fall in love with this beauty? "He must if he's asked ye to marry him. What has he said to ye about it?"

"Nothing."

He sat up, knowing Heather must not be understanding what he meant. "Has he never complimented ye?"

She nodded. "He usually says I look pretty."

"And?"

"Sometimes he says I look very pretty." She looked as though she was starting to fret. "Should there be more?"

Aye, breathtaking. Spectacular. Beautiful. Magical.

"Perhaps once ye're married and can spend time alone, he'll tell ye how he truly feels. There is no' much a man can say to ye when ye're always in a crowd. Especially one as well-heeled as his circle of friends." Although what would it have taken for Tilbury to steal a moment and whisper sweet nothings in Heather's ear? Or talk about anything that crossed his mind. Did he not wish to share his thoughts and feelings with his own betrothed?

"Yes, I'm sure he will."

Robbie had never heard anyone sound more uncertain. "Pixie, has he even kissed ye yet?"

She raised her hand and pointed to it. "Yes, often. He bows over my outstretched hand and kisses it ardently. Not in any slobbering way…just, with feeling."

"And?"

"Then he sets it down, and we might talk for a while, or he asks me to dance. Usually, he asks me to save a waltz and the supper dance for him. Robbie, why are you rolling your eyes at me? And why are your lips pinched? You look like you just ate a toad."

He raked a hand through his hair. "Ye are betrothed to the man, and he has never kissed ye on the lips?"

"Should he have? Isn't it frowned upon before one is married?

More than frowned upon, in truth. It's been pounded into my brain since I began tutoring for my come-out. Never kiss a man. A corollary to that is never be alone with a man. Although you and I are alone but out in the open. I suppose that does not count since I'm sure Uncle John and Uncle George are spying on us. Why are you frowning, Robbie?"

"He wants to marry ye, and he hasn't kissed ye? And are ye saying he dinna claim the privilege once ye were betrothed? I dinna like it, Heather. Not at all. He should be wild with frustration and desperate to taste yer lips. I would have kissed ye."

"Then why haven't you?"

"I'm not the one offering to marry ye." But he ached to kiss her something fierce. Not just kiss her. Hold her. Love her. Protect her. Spend his entire life with her.

A soldier's life, which meant no life for her. He was right back where he started. Wanting her and knowing he was completely wrong for her.

"Should I take him aside before the ball and require him to kiss me?"

"Dinna ask me that," he said with a growl.

She tossed the book aside. "This is pointless. You would have kissed me, and he should have kissed me, but I shouldn't ask him to kiss me? You've read this book. You know what it says. But you're not helping me to understand it. All you're doing is speaking in riddles. And my sisters, as much as I adore them, are also no help."

"They told ye to read the book."

"They told me to read it with *you*. Why? Because they hope we'll fall in love with each other? Then you, Joshua, and Ronan can all remain best friends married to the Yorkshire Farthingale sisters, namely me, Holly, and Dahlia. One big happy family. That's a big waste of time, isn't it?"

"Aye, it is. But not for the reason ye think."

"I do know the reason." She tipped her chin up in indignation. "Isn't it obvious? You don't love me. You think I'm childish and spoiled, and let us not forget ignorant because I don't know anything about anything. I make a laughable debutante. And now you think I'll make an unworthy marchioness."

He snorted. "If ye'd read the book, ye'd know that is bollocks. Even if ye were all that, which ye're not, how is my behavior any better? When was the last time ye took a drunken dive off a wall?"

"Never." She laughed lightly but then quickly turned serious. "Then what is the truth? I wish someone would just come straight out and tell me. My family seems to have chosen you as the bearer of these bad tidings. So just tell me already. What is going on? What am I supposed to know that I don't know?"

He took her hand when he saw it was trembling. "They are concerned you and Tilbury do no' love each other sufficiently to sustain a happy marriage."

"What is that supposed to mean?"

"There's no passion between ye, lass. Do ye think Joshua could have ever kept his hands off Holly? And what about Ronan and Dahlia? Only a supreme idiot or a man in love would have ridden for hours with damaged ribs to return to London and the woman he loves."

"Tilbury has had no reason to test his love. I've never been in danger. I have no madman after me. It's just an ordinary courtship. Well, not ordinary…but he's been raised to be a gentleman and has had a noble sense of duty ingrained in him. He isn't a military man, not used to leading a cavalry charge or seizing the high ground in battle. I don't know that he has ever faced death or ever felt a sense of dire urgency. It isn't fair to compare him to other men."

"Pixie, but that's just it. Stripped down to our essence, we are all the same. King, marquess, soldier, or commoner. We are compelled by the same primitive urges to find our mate, the one we will love and protect from wolves, and breed offspring."

"And this is why he is described as a man of *noble* breeding. Because he does not look at me that way. Nor does his family. I've met his mother and sister, and they like me."

"I'm sure they like boiled potatoes, too."

She yanked her hand from his grasp. "Are you calling me a boiled potato?"

"No. Och, lass. It's complicated."

"Apparently so, because everyone thinks I'm too dimwitted to figure it out."

"We're all too dimwitted. None of us has yet to figure out what makes a person fall in love. Ye're young and inexperienced. I've had years of experience, and still dinna know what the hell I'm doing. But this isn't about me. It's about yer future and happiness."

At this point, a man with any brains would have admitted he loved her. But he had no brains when it came to Heather. He loved her to the depths of his soul and also knew to the depths of his soul they were wrong for each other. She'd be so unhappy in Caithness, and it would ruin any hope of their love surviving.

He decided to move on to a discussion of the next chapters. These were safer...he hoped. "Ye've read far enough into the book to know that we use our five senses to form our attraction to each other. Sight. Touch. Taste. Scent. Hearing."

"I've only read as far as sight and touch."

"The concept is the same for each sense. It isn't so much what they are, but how you open yerself up to seeing what's really before ye. It's all about not lying to yerself and pretending ye see whatever it is ye want to see. So, let's start with the look of Tilbury. What do ye like about him, lass? I mean, physically. We'll get to the other qualities later. Name five things ye like about the look of him."

He waited for her response.

And waited some more.

Hellfire, what was going on?

42

Couldn't Heather come up with five things she liked about the man she was determined to marry?

"*Heether*," he said, his brogue more pronounced to reflect his concern. "Lass, can ye name one?"

CHAPTER FIVE

HEATHER FROWNED AT Robbie. "Of course I can think of five things I like about Tilbury. He has a pleasant face. He is elegant. His hair is not falling out."

"Gad, I can see he's swept ye off yer feet." He rolled his eyes. "That's three, lass. Why did ye stop?"

"He is tall, although not quite as tall as you."

"I'm sure there's Viking blood mixed in with the MacLauren bloodlines. Ye're almost there. Can ye think of one more thing ye like about this marquess ye intend to marry?"

"Why are you being such an oaf to me? He has nice eyes and a nice smile. There, that makes *six* in all."

He sighed. "Lass, ye could have been describing yer dance instructor from five years ago for all the passion ye've shown in yer description of him."

She clenched her hands. "Passion? Everyone tosses that word about as though it is something sinful to experience before marriage. How am I supposed to understand passion when I've never even been kissed?"

"So why hasn't he used his prerogative and kissed ye?"

Her head began to spin.

She already lacked self-assurance, and Robbie's comments were only making her feel worse. Yes, Tilbury ought to have kissed her by now. What hadn't he? "I don't know why he hasn't bothered to kiss me yet," she replied in a shaky breath. "But why would he ask me to marry him unless he liked me? I bring nothing else to the marriage."

He groaned, his eyes now filled with pity.

"What should I do, Robbie? You're the one with experience. Do I insist on a kiss? Would he regard it as too forward of me?"

"Go with what yer heart tells ye is right, lass. It isn't fair of me to provoke feelings in ye that ye've been taught to deny. This would not concern me if ye were of a mind to marry for purposes of advancing alliances. But it is well known that ye Farthingale lasses will only marry for love."

She nodded. "My family is considered odd for encouraging it."

He studied her in a way that made the butterflies in her stomach flutter. "I think they have the right of it, if ye care for my opinion."

"Will you marry for love, Robbie?"

"Not likely. My granduncle will arrange a marriage for me, I expect. He's quite pleased with the match Malcolm made, marrying the Earl of Wycke's sister. That's a love match for certain, although he and Malcolm were, in fact, pushing for an alliance and nothing more."

"But your brother fell in love with his wife?"

"From the moment he set eyes on her. I never thought any woman could tame him. I was sure his perfect match would be a firebrand, someone as stubborn as he can be, and not afraid to hurl a jug at his head to keep him in line. But Anne, she's a quiet thing. Sweet. Never shouts, yet has the mettle to hold her ground whenever Malcolm gets pigheaded about something."

"I don't think Tilbury has a temper. He always seems to be in control. How would I know if I love him, Robbie? What should I be feeling?"

He closed his eyes as he leaned back to soak in the sunshine on his face. "I canno' say. Everyone responds differently. Everyone looks for different things in a mate. This is where the five senses come in. For example, the look of ye. Some men may be attracted to tall blondes with big breasts...sorry, lass. Just saying. Some men like a handful of flesh they can grab onto."

"And you?"

"Does no' matter what I like. We're talking about you and Tilbury. Obviously, he likes little pixies like you. Ye're not all that little. Just average height, but ye have a light, graceful step, and there is a fey quality about ye that he must find enchanting or he would no' be bothering with ye."

"It must be love for his part, because why else would he offer for me? I am not an advantageous match for alliance purposes. He seems to like me, and we always have a nice time when we are together." She nibbled her lip. "But if passion is a fiery thing, then...do I set him on fire? If so, he is very good at hiding his feelings. Or am I very bad at noticing what he is feeling?"

"Probably a mix of both. He hides his passion, and ye're too inexperienced to know what telltale signs to look for in a man."

"I am woefully inexperienced. I readily admit it. This is why my sisters think I am still an ignorant child."

"And yet, ye're the one who got the marriage proposal from a marquess." Robbie frowned at her. "Is it that important to ye, lass? Are ye mistaking yer love for the title as love for the man himself?"

This question should not have shaken her to the core, but it did. "I don't know, Robbie. I hope not."

"This is why ye've been afraid to read the book. Ye don't wish to find out the truth."

She felt her eyes begin to tear, but she fought to hold them back. "Our parents raised us to be a helpmate and consort to someone important. What else am I good for, if not that? I don't have Dahlia's artistic talents. My cousin Rose is also a brilliant artist. Laurel is a respected horse breeder. Lily is a scientist. Violet has one of the finest singing voices in England. But me? Nothing."

"Dinna say that. Ye're young still."

"No younger than my cousins were when they reached for their dreams. The only dream I ever had was to marry a marquess. How's that for a shallow, self-serving goal?"

"Dinna be hard on yerself. Ye'd be an asset to Tilbury as his marchioness. As he gets to know ye better, he'll learn to respect yer opinions. Obviously, he sees something in ye that he does no' see in any other female."

"But what is that reason? Does he see a biddable idiot?"

"No. Why would any man wish to marry a fool? Which ye're not."

"Then what is the reason? This is what I am struggling to understand. I am not a wealthy heiress. I am not a lady of rank. And he has not been passionate in his declarations to me. So, what does he see in me to make him choose me?"

Robbie took a deep breath. "This is why the chapters on the five senses are so important. Whatever he sees in ye, the sight of ye. The scent of ye. The lovely touch of ye. The sweet lilt of yer voice. This is what makes ye perfect for him."

"You've only mentioned four senses."

"Well, he has no' kissed ye yet. I dinna mean kissed yer hand, although he probably liked the taste of yer skin. It isn't quite the same as a kiss on the lips."

She stared at her hands that were now clenched and resting on her lap. "Robbie, did you ever desire to kiss me?"

He said nothing for the longest time, to the point she believed he was going to ignore the question. Then he groaned lightly and said, "Yes, I did."

She glanced up, startled. "Because you have a strongly defined low brain?"

By the scathing look he shot her, she realized she'd insulted him. "I told ye, ye're not a low brain lass for me. Ye never were and never will be."

She stared at him, and he stared back, neither one of them blinking or turning away. What was he telling her? That if not for Tilbury, he would have courted her?

She tore her gaze away from him and looked up at the sky. It was blue and clear, not a storm cloud to be seen. The air was dry, and the breeze was gentle. But it felt as though a lightning bolt had suddenly struck between them, leaving the air thick and charged.

Her heart began to beat a little faster. "Robbie, was there ever a time you thought I was the one for you? That you could love me?"

What would she do if he said yes? She truly did not know. She had never believed he could...

But what if she was wrong?

No.

Robbie had only to crook his finger, and a hundred ladies would come running. Why ever would he single her out?

Time seemed to suspend between them.

He emitted another soft groan. "Dinna say a word until ye hear me out completely, *Heether*."

Here it was, he was going to let her down gently. He did not love her. But he did not wish to hurt her feelings since his two best friends had fallen madly in love with her sisters. So he wanted to be polite and try his best not to insult her.

Her heart had now shot into her throat as she waited for his brutally honest assessment. She was a respectable girl, and he did not wish to malign her. Was this what he meant when he'd said he had only ever regarded her with his high brain, never his low brain? "All right. Just be truthful with me, Robbie."

"I will, lass." He took a deep breath before pressing on. It seemed to be a painful struggle for him to exhale. "If I ever allowed myself to love, ye'd be the one I could love."

She gasped.

"No, Heather. Hear me out. I dinna need to read that book to know I could have feelings for ye." He held up a hand when she opened her mouth to respond. "No, lass. There's more. It's important ye listen to all I have to say first."

She nodded, barely able to concentrate after his admission. He loved her? Was it possible?

"What I told ye earlier was the truth. I looked at ye differently from the first. Ye were never just another female to conquer."

"Why did you never tell me this before? Why did you disappear for months and never let me know your feelings?"

"Because I have no feelings. It is a luxury I canno' afford." He cleared his throat. "Malcolm, that's my brother, is heir to the Earl of Caithness. I am nothing."

"Robbie! How dare you think of yourself as—"

"Lass, I dinna mean that I am worthless. All I mean is that I have nothing to offer ye but my heart. In a perfect world, this might be enough. But how can it ever be enough for ye after the way ye've been raised and the expectations ye've got in yer head? Ye'll understand it better when ye read the chapter about our damn expectations and how they can destroy our chance at happiness."

"It's in the book?"

"Aye, lass. We'll get to it later. The point I am trying to make is, would ye toss away a marquess to live on the wages of a cavalry captain?"

"I don't need to live like a queen."

"That is no' all. As my wife, ye'd be expected to live in Caithness, because even though I'm just a captain in the Scots Greys, I am also the earl's grandnephew. Not the heir, but nonetheless expected to make my home there. He has no children, so Malcolm and I were raised as though we were his own sons."

He spared her a glance and continued. "We're a Highland clan, but so far north, it would take almost a fortnight's ride south just to reach Edinburgh. It would take a month to reach London, assuming good weather most of the way. So how can I ask ye to leave yer family and lead a solitary existence with me? I dinna even know how much time I'd be spending with ye, for I'm still in military service and can be sent anywhere in the world on a moment's notice."

"But you were the Scottish liaison to Parliament. Why can you not stay on in that role?"

"Because my home is in Caithness. I dinna like being here in London. But you do. Yer place is here."

"I grew up in York."

His expression remained mirthless. "Ye're flourishing here in London. If I brought ye to Caithness, yer heart would wither and die. We both know it. This is why ye refused to read the book with me until today. So, let's have no more discussion about *us*, because we are not meant to be."

She rolled to her knees, her hands clenched and her head ready to explode. She was so angry. "Who appointed you the Lord High Judge? Do I not get a say in this?"

He remained unmoved. "Ye did have a say, lass. Ye chose to ignore yer promise to yer sisters. I waited around for ye to stop hiding and finally come around to reading the book with me. Ye never did. Ye just kept shoving it back at me. So I took it and rode off."

Heather felt her insides crumbling.

Everything he'd said was right. She had wanted to marry her marquess so badly, she'd broken her promise to her sisters. She'd lied to herself in every possible way. It was all catching up to her now. The worst part was that in disappointing everyone she cared about, she'd also destroyed any possible future with Robbie.

She had chosen the marquess over him, and he was never going to forgive her.

And yet, his assessment was right.

What life would there be for her in Caithness, especially if she were to spend months and possibly years alone while he was away on assignment? This was the life Violet had accepted, but she was here in

London with lots of family to support her. And Romulus was so different from Robbie. He loved Violet deeply, and everyone saw it and felt it to their bones.

But Robbie? Was he capable of being faithful to his wife? Even if forced to spend years apart?

"Lass," he said with a wrenching groan, "dinna shed tears. We both know ye made the right choice. So why don't we just finish this up fast? Let's concentrate on yer marquess and all the reasons he'll make ye happy."

"All right." The only problem was her secret dreams had been filled with Robbie ever since meeting him. He was the hero she always conjured up in the dark of night when the truth spilled out. He was the romantic hero her thoughts skittered to whenever she read one of those scandalous books she was never allowed to read. Of course, she inhaled them voraciously because they were prohibited.

She did not know why it was Robbie and not Tilbury, who appeared in her dreams and waking fantasies. Perhaps because marriage to the marquess was real and Robbie was only meant to be just that, a reckless fantasy. "I cannot be without ye, lass," he would say in his husky, Highland brogue, and crush his lips to hers. She would respond, of course, running her hands along his warm skin and the bulging muscles they covered...because shirtless, Robbie was a thing of beauty, and that's how she dreamed of him.

Virile and splendid.

His body hard and smooth, as though carved from ancient rock.

Lately, her dreams had grown quite torrid. Robbie kissing her lips, her throat. Robbie wrapping her in his arms and running his big hands over her body. As for herself, she was encouraging him in these rapturous fantasies, lost to all reason, even when common sense ought to have made her wake up.

Everything about him was perfection, in a beautiful and masculine way.

"Pixie, what are ye thinking?"

"You won't like it, Robbie."

"Try me," he said softly.

"Well, I warned you. The thing is…I think it is important for me to know. Perhaps to have a suitable comparison. How else would I know if it was good or not?"

He regarded her, utterly confused. "What is it ye wish to know?"

"What the right kiss feels like."

He inhaled sharply.

"Do you think we might share one kiss? You and me. On the lips. Then I would know and not spend the rest of my life wondering."

"Pixie, no. It is a very bad idea."

"Robbie, please. One kiss, and then we'll be done with each other forever."

"Done? Forever? Ye truly think so, lass?"

She nodded.

"Are ye daft? Ye'd give away yer first kiss to me?"

Oh, sweet mercy.

Did he now believe she was carelessly giving away her favors? He had every reason to believe so since she had been careless about reading *The Book of Love*. It sat there on the blanket between them, and she wanted to rip it to pieces and toss it in the dustbin. It was supposed to be an enchanted book, but it was only bringing her a massive headache.

And an equally massive heartache.

She tipped her head in indignation. "Then forget I asked. Obviously, it was a mistake. One of the many you believe I've made. Stupidly, I thought it could be something we'd each treasure since it would be the only thing we'd ever have of each other. But why should *you* think this way? This is my first kiss, but probably your hundredth or even thousandth."

Despite trying to maintain a semblance of pride, she failed at that, too. Her heart was breaking, and she could not stop these feelings of loss and sadness from overwhelming her. "Robbie, I can't do this. It hurts too much."

He rose and drew her up with him, wrapping his arms around her and holding her so gently it only made her want to cry. "I know, lass. And ye think I've insulted ye. I dinna mean it that way. I'd be honored to be yer first kiss. No kiss before or after would ever be sweeter for me."

She closed her eyes tightly and just breathed him in. He always smelled nice, a hint of musk and spice. Even earlier, while reeking of ale and cheap perfume, beneath it all was the clean, masculine scent of him.

She was pressed to his hard body. Perhaps she was the one pressing herself against him. She no longer cared if he believed her foolish and wanton. All that mattered to her now was to be swallowed in his embrace and held for as long as he would allow.

They stood beside the shade tree, only Robbie had moved them over so that the trunk of the tree hid them from view of everyone in the house. How long before her uncles came running out? Of course, this assumed they had not grown bored and stopped watching them. After all, Violet also had to be grabbing their attention.

What a mess.

Violet in labor.

Romulus not arrived yet.

Heather understood the nature of these Brayden men and knew Romulus would never forgive himself for not being here to protect his wife, no matter that both families were taking up the slack.

Would anyone care about Tilbury's ball this evening? Suddenly, it did not feel exciting to celebrate her impending marriage to a marquess who had not even kissed her.

And here she was, willing to give up her precious first kiss to Robbie, knowing full well he would never agree to marry her.

"Heether," he said in a rough whisper, his lips pressed close to her ear. "We dinna have to do this, lass."

Yes, they did.

She took his face in her hands and brought his head down to hers. "We do, Robbie. There'll be a gaping hole in my heart where that memory would have been stored if we don't. Please, kiss me."

He looked as though he wanted to crawl into a hole and die in there. "Promise me ye'll no' regret it."

"I promise you," she said with a nod. "I shall never regret a single moment of your lips on mine." She closed her eyes, puckered her lips, and waited...and waited some more...and finally opened her eyes again.

His expression was fathomless.

"Robbie, what are you doing?"

"Wondering how I'm ever going to forget ye," he said, drawing her up hard against him and capturing her lips with exquisite gentleness, and at the same time, an exquisite heat. No one ever doubted this big Scot knew how to kiss a girl and turn her brains to pudding.

He caught her lips, trapped them, teased them, and claimed them for his own.

She'd read those scandalous passages in novels where the heroine surrendered to the hero. *She was helpless to resist.* Those were the words often used to describe the power of the hero's kiss. This is how she felt now, utterly helpless, and craving more of Robbie.

He had only to touch his lips to hers, and she was conquered, eager for his plunder...well, he was only plundering her mouth.

Merciful heaven.

She did not think she would resist him if he sought more.

Fire shot through her blood, spreading the flames to her limbs and bones. The kiss continued, hot and sweet. Seemingly endless, and at the same time, she ached because it would soon end.

But not yet.

His lips ground against hers, not brutally but with a forceful gentleness. She felt his ravenous longing, his fierce desperation to taste every morsel, savor every memory of her. She felt the same for him. This is all they would ever have of each other.

He left nothing of her untouched, not her heart nor her soul.

She wrapped her arms around his neck and dug her fingers in his hair, his beautiful mane of burnished gold. She was practically climbing up the front of him in her need to touch him, to feel the heat of his muscled body. The rough pads of his fingers traced along her skin with a feathery softness that made her quiver.

She wanted every drop and dram of this big, beautiful Scot and ached in the knowledge there would be nothing more.

One kiss wasn't nearly enough. How could she tell him?

They'd agreed. This was to be all they would have of each other.

This memory would have to sustain them until they took their last breath.

He slipped his tongue between the seam of her lips and began to explore her mouth, slowly swirling and tangling it with hers. Then he tore his lips off hers. "Pixie, *blessed saints.*"

His hands slipped under her ribs, hinting of something wonderful if only he would move them upward. Just the littlest bit higher. But they held there, to her frustration.

He refused to take the next step and cup her breast.

It made little sense to her since her breasts were already pillowed against his chest, tightly pressed to him as she absorbed the heat and strength of him. But somehow, to this proud Scot, touching her there would have taken their kiss a step too far.

He meant to give her a first kiss, which was an altogether different undertaking than a first grope.

What did it say about her that she desired everything from him? Her five senses were in an uproar, swirling around her, striking her all at once so that she felt dazed and reeling. The handsome look of him.

His exquisite touch. The divine taste of his lips. The scent of his masculine heat, intoxicating and turning her into a wild, wanton thing, no better than an ewe in heat. His soft, husky growl of satisfaction.

She tried to restore the pieces of her broken heart as he eased her out of his embrace. "Pixie, ye're trembling."

Try as she might, she could not stop. He had to know their kiss had shaken the very foundations of her soul.

"Och, lass. This was a terrible mistake."

"A mistake?" Not for her. It was beautiful and perfect and a memory she would always treasure. But she nodded, realizing he must not have felt this same perfection. Measured against all the girls he'd kissed, hers had to be inept and among the worst. "It was my first time. I tried my best. In my own defense, you overwhelmed me."

"That is no' what I meant." He ran a hand through his hair. "I have to go."

She stared at him, startled. "But we haven't finished reading the book."

His gaze was hot enough to engulf both of them in flames. "I dinna think I can help ye any further. Read it, lass. Finish it today if ye can. I'll be leaving London tonight."

Her heart shot into her throat. "Why, Robbie? You have to stay until my wedding. Oh, heavens. What am I saying? What am I doing? My wedding. And I kissed *you*."

"I know, lass. It is not a proud moment for either of us. Send word to me at my granduncle's townhouse if ye have something ye wish to tell me. But do it quickly. I'll no' be here by nightfall."

"Nightfall?" Her head was spinning. "No, it's too soon. What can I say to change your mind? Must I beg you to stay?" *Merciful heavens.* She had been reduced to begging him.

"Why would ye do that?" He reached out and ran his thumb lightly across her lower lip. "What would ye have me stay here for?"

For you.

For us.

THE HEART OF LOVE

But he'd just told her their kiss was a mistake.

He'd spent the morning going over all the reasons why their love, should he ever allow himself to love her—which he wouldn't—would never last.

Not only would it not last, but it would be a horrific disaster.

This kiss was all he needed and the last contact he ever wanted from her.

He waited for an answer she was terrified to give. "Right, lass. I thought so." He gave her a whisper-soft kiss on the cheek. "I wish ye a happy life with yer marquess."

CHAPTER SIX

ROBBIE HAD MEANT to return to the Caithness residence, pack up his belongings, and leave London before the Tilbury ball. He had to leave now because if he remained a moment longer, he was going to attend that ball and likely wreck it.

But the Fates were working against him, as though purposely tossing objects in his path to delay him. First, Gallant had thrown a shoe that had to be replaced. As soon as his trusted gray had been properly shod, Robbie had returned to the house to retrieve his travel pouches, only to find he had received a summons from Lord Liverpool. He was commanded to meet England's top minister at Westminster Hall at four o'clock this afternoon. "Bollocks, what does he want?"

He arrived at the appointed hour, impatient to learn what the summons was about, give some glib response, and then be on his way north before something else arose to interfere with his plans.

Leaving this late in the day, he would not make it very far before darkness fell. But he did not care. He only needed to be out of London and away from the temptation of seeing Heather again.

His legs felt like lead weights as he strode into Liverpool's office. Lord Liverpool rose from his chair behind the large mahogany table that served as his desk and came around to greet him. "MacLauren," he said, sounding not at all jovial, "your replacement is an arse."

"Dinna I tell ye that when ye first chose him? Not even the Scots like him, and he's one of ours." Robbie folded his arms across his chest, a gesture that was most certainly disrespectful. He no longer cared. He wanted to be out of London. "But how is this my problem?"

He received a scathing frown in response. "Because I am making it your problem."

"How? And what if I refuse to be dragged into your politics? I'm about to return to Caithness."

"No, you're not. And I am not asking you. I am commanding you."

Robbie shook his head, not quite certain where this discussion was headed, but he already knew it was not going in a direction to his liking. "And just what are ye commanding me to do?"

"You are to return to your position as the military liaison. Mac-Donald is out. You're back in."

"Over my dead body."

"Fine, if it has to be that way. Stop behaving like a bloody, stub-born Scot. Were all of you born with a thistle stuck up your arse to make you so contrary? If you attempt to flee London, I shall send an entire dragoon regiment after you. They'll have orders to shoot you if you resist."

His heart sank into his stomach. "Ye canno' do this."

"Indeed, I can." Liverpool motioned for him to take a chair. "Who's to stop me?"

No one could, Robbie realized and grudgingly sat down. A damn horseshoe and now this. All he wanted to do was get out of London so that Heather could marry her marquess and be happy for the rest of her life. How was this wrong?

He sat forward in his chair and groaned. "How long must I stay?"

Liverpool's demeanor softened as he resumed his own seat behind the desk. "One month. Maybe two. Sooner if you can find me another MacLauren to take over as liaison. I want a man with brains, not a hot-tempered, drunken buffoon who believes he is Robert the Bruce reincarnated."

Robbie cast him an 'I told ye so' look. "I warned ye about appointing a MacDonald to the post."

"The choice wasn't mine alone to make."

"Spreading the blame now? This is what ye politicians do best. Ye made yer choice. Why can ye no' live with it?"

"Your Scottish earls also had input. So did my cabinet."

Robbie arched an eyebrow. "Seems to me, ye ought to sack yer cabinet."

Liverpool cast him a wry smile. "Stop flinging the problem in my face. Believe me, I've considered sacking the lot of them more than once. MacLauren, I know you wish to return to Caithness. I promise you, this will only be a temporary assignment. It is the best I can do for you at the moment. We're done now."

He rose to signal the end of their meeting. "But it is good to see you again. You'll have your old office back, of course. Let me know if there is anything you need. Welcome home, son. You were sorely missed."

He ought to have been flattered, but all he felt was irritation while he rode back to the Caithness residence.

Bollocks.

His home was in the Highlands, not bloody London.

And what was he to do about Heather? He'd meant the one kiss he'd shared with her to be the end of any further contact between them. He needed to put a stop to whatever it was that simmered between them.

Not merely stop it but stamp it out. Crush it. Stuff it into the deepest recesses of his heart and never allow the feeling to see the light of day while he had breath left in him.

One thing for bloody certain, he was not going to attend Tilbury's ball. Why torture himself by watching his pixie dance with her betrothed?

"Over and done," he muttered, knowing he had fulfilled his obligations and more. He'd read the book with Heather…most of it…enough of it.

He'd given her a first kiss, which would also be their last.

Bollocks again.

He had not expected it to be so good.

Of course, he'd known what he was doing. But she had never been kissed before, and didn't even know how to pucker her lips properly. And yet, it was the best kiss he'd ever received. It left him ravenous for more. Only there could never be more.

He undressed and washed, intending to retire early and drink himself senseless while alone in his bedchamber. He hadn't the heart to go out drinking with friends or sit in on a game of cards. He hadn't the desire to ease his frustration with a woman, no matter that he could have any of his choosing…just not Heather.

He sank onto his bed, clad only in a towel, and clutching a bottle of bootleg whisky in his hand. It was a family brew carried down from generation to generation and would burn out the guts of a lesser man. But the MacLauren men had been weaned on it, so it was mother's milk to them.

Still, taking to bed with a bottle and drinking himself into a stupor was probably a new low for him. He could blame it on his arm, a necessary liquid salve to numb the pain since it was sore from the stitches he'd received earlier. After bathing, he'd rubbed more unguent on the wound as Dr. Farthingale had instructed and then bandaged it again.

He was about to open the bottle when he heard footsteps on the stairs. *Blessed Scottish saints.* Who had Crawford let in now?

"Och, what are ye two lunkheads doing here?" he muttered as Joshua and Ronan marched in, dressed in their properly elegant evening wear instead of their usual uniforms. Joshua was a captain in the King's First Dragoon Guards, and Ronan was a captain in the

Royal Navy. They'd shed their usual regalia for formal black jackets and snow-white vests and ties. "Why are ye two here? What did ye do with yer wives?"

"Holly and Dahlia went on ahead with Lady Miranda," Joshua said, referring to his and Ronan's flame-haired mother. The woman had the heart of a warrior and could scare the wits out of an army of a thousand men.

"Why did ye no' go with them?"

Ronan cast him an all too merry grin. "Because our wives told us to come here first and get you. So here we are. Don't get too comfortable. You're coming with us to Tilbury's ball."

"The hell I will." He scowled at both of them. "Is this what ye've descended to? Lackeys for yer wives? Sniveling, groveling cowards afraid to contradict them? I am no' going to that affair. Go back and tell them ye couldn't find me. I was no' at home."

"No. Sorry, Robbie." Joshua held out his hands in supplication. "First, they'd know we were lying. Don't ask me how, they'd just pick up on it. You'd think lies carried a scent, and they could sniff them out like bloodhounds with their delicate noses."

Robbie was not going to give in. "Are they looking to disrupt Heather's betrothal? Because that is what will happen if I show up. Not for my part, but for Heather's. She's already twisted in knots over Tilbury. Why are Holly and Dahlia pushing her? Do they no' realize they are only hurting their sister?"

"They are trying to save her," Joshua said.

"From what? Marrying the man of her dreams?"

"But we all know he isn't," Ronan said. "Don't you think it is odd that none of us have noticed even a glimmer of passion between them? I'm not saying Tilbury should be trying to seduce her, but he isn't even tempted to steal a kiss. This is what worries our wives."

Robbie arched an eyebrow. "He's a marquess. He knows how to be discreet about such things."

"My arse," Joshua said. "There's discretion, and then there's just…I don't even know what it is those two are doing. I understand Heather's reasons. As you said, she's been dreaming of marrying a marquess ever since she was a little girl. But Tilbury? What does he want with her? Have you ever considered that? We've all been putting our attention on Heather and never once bothered to question Tilbury's motives."

"It isn't a question of sexual persuasion," Ronan added. "We know he likes women, but this troubles Holly and Dahlia all the more. Why hasn't he touched Heather? I think it's time we dug into his motives. Don't you?"

Robbie's gut churned.

They were right, damn it.

He hadn't thought about Tilbury, just assumed the man was as enchanted by Heather as he was. But to not even kiss her? What was going on in Tilbury's head? If there were no business reasons to form a marriage alliance, and he wasn't in love with the lass, then why marry her? "Ye need say no more. I'll come with ye."

He set aside the bottle and hurriedly dressed, his friends serving as valets to help him along.

Within the hour, he, Joshua, and Ronan strode into Tilbury's ballroom. They had arrived late, and the dancing had already started. In truth, Robbie was relieved. His heart could not have withstood watching Heather open the dance with her marquess. He could not bear the thought of another man holding her in his arms. "Och, I see them. There's Tilbury. He's standing with the Duke of Stoke, Dahlia, and Heather."

Joshua peeled away from them. "I see Holly talking to her cousins, Rose and Daisy. I'll see you gentlemen later. Don't be an arse, Robbie. Mind your manners."

He'd been dealing with politicians for the past year. He knew how to be tactful…when he wanted to be. But as he and Ronan approached their party, Robbie realized the other young lady with Dahlia was not Heather, but Stoke's daughter, Lady Melinda.

Gad, from the back, she and Heather looked so much alike.

To Robbie's surprise, Stoke greeted him as though they were long-lost friends. "MacLauren, I hear you're back in your old position. Thank the Graces! It's good to have you back, son. I've never met a bigger bag of hot air than your replacement. He singlehandedly did more for Scottish secession than all the clan leaders put together. The man was so odious, we were willing to do anything to be rid of him."

Tilbury laughed good-naturedly. "It's nice to see you back, MacLauren. I second Stoke's opinion."

Robbie politely greeted the ladies and tried not to be obvious in searching for Heather. He eased when he noticed her dancing with her uncle, Rupert Farthingale. He remained with his host and their small group since Rupert would return Heather here once the dance had ended. He tried not to yawn as he listened to Dahlia and Lady Melinda describe the remodeling work underway in Stoke's residence.

Ronan and Tilbury appeared fascinated, so he let them comment while he stayed silent and merely nodded on occasion to let them believe he had not fallen asleep on his feet from sheer boredom.

"Dahlia has been assisting my daughter in redoing our entire house," Stoke told him, suddenly becoming Robbie's best friend. "It started as one small project in my study. But we were all so pleased with the results, we decided to expand the project to the music room and guest parlor."

Lady Melinda was smiling and nodding vigorously. "We've been having so much fun. We are now redoing our entire home. Captain Brayden," she said, addressing Ronan, "your wife is a gem. We adore her."

Ronan grinned at Dahlia. "I'm rather fond of her, too."

Lady Melinda laughed. "It is quite obvious to all of us and quite understandable. She has a lovely way of dealing with me and my father, somehow quietly winning out—and correctly so—even when we stubbornly disagree with her."

Stoke emitted a bark of laughter. "I'm sure she leads you around by the nose, Brayden, and you don't even know it."

"Oh, I know it. I simply don't mind," Ronan admitted with a chuckle, casting Dahlia another doting glance.

The dance was ending, and Robbie suddenly realized Heather did not know he'd be attending. She had been overset earlier today, with good reason. He should never have kissed her and certainly should not have put his heart into the kiss. How would she respond upon seeing him now?

He turned to the ladies. "Would you care for some champagne?"

They both accepted his offer with a nod of gratitude.

He left before Heather spied him.

In any event, he preferred to watch her and Tilbury from a distance to catch them in unguarded moments. Botheration, he liked Tilbury. His instincts were usually excellent, and nothing alarmed him about the man.

Perhaps there was nothing at all sinister in his motives. Farthingales married for love, but who was to say Tilbury wanted the upheaval that love often brought? Was it possible he preferred a pleasant companion and not an ardent bed partner? But did this mean he'd take his passion elsewhere? It would destroy Heather to learn her husband had taken on a mistress.

He shook his head.

Tilbury was not known for this sort of behavior. He wasn't one to take on mistresses.

"Damn it." He needed to figure out the man before Heather married him. He grabbed three glasses of champagne now that Heather had returned to their small group. She would likely be thirsty after that last dance.

He hoped Ronan had the sense to drop a hint he was here, prepare

Heather for the surprise of seeing him again. The lass had an expressive face. He was already concerned about the kiss they should not have shared. Stoke and Tilbury were not fools. One wrong look on her part, and they would realize what had happened between them.

He purposely approached from an angle where he could put his body between Heather and everyone else, hoping she would only need a few seconds to adjust to the unexpected sight of him.

"Miss Farthingale, I thought ye might be thirsty after the dance and brought ye a glass of champagne. Forgive my presumption, but I had offered the other ladies and did not wish to leave ye out. Or would ye prefer a different libation?"

She was staring at him, those big eyes of hers a window into her heart. She was showing every blessed feeling now coursing through her. Surprise, hurt, confusion, and a host of more dangerous expressions. Joy, relief, desire…love.

Blessed saints.

His heart was now in palpitations, and his expression probably revealed too much. He couldn't help it; she was so beautiful. He supposed it was a good thing he had his back to the others. Heather wasn't the only one unable to hide thoughts.

"Thank you, Captain MacLauren," she said in a tremulous whisper. "I am thirsty. Most kind of you to think of me."

She grabbed the glass from his hand and guzzled its contents down like a sailor on his first shore leave.

There was little he could do about it, not while holding the other two champagne glasses. He now turned to Dahlia and Lady Melinda to hand them their drinks, cringing at the thought of what Heather might do next. When he turned back to her, he saw that her cheeks were bright pink, and she looked overheated. He hoped the others would mistake her heightened color as heat exhaustion from her last dance and not what it truly was, the flush of desire.

He often received such looks, women desiring him for his body.

He was never particularly affected one way or the other. If he were in the mood, he would subtly signal back, and they'd go off and do the deed. But Heather was nothing like these other women. She wasn't asking for his body. Nor was she offering hers.

She was offering him her heart.

Not that she understood what she was doing…or knew what she was feeling.

He wanted to wrap her in his arms.

Tilbury was now staring at her. "My dear, are you unwell?"

She returned her betrothed's stare with mounting panic. "What?"

"Ye look as though ye might need a bit of air, Miss Farthingale," Robbie interjected. "It is obvious the dancing tired ye out, and the champagne did not sit well with ye."

She nodded. "I drank it too fast."

The music struck up again. Tilbury regarded her in dismay. "I've promised this waltz to Lady Melinda. But we can…"

"No, you must dance. Please do. I'll be fine in a moment. My sister and Captain Brayden can escort me outdoors. I do need a little air."

Tilbury and Lady Melinda appeared reluctant but finally agreed at Heather's insistence. That left only Stoke with them.

To Robbie's irritation, Stoke offered Heather his arm. "Come, my dear. We shall all take a turn on the veranda. Are you joining us, MacLauren?"

The man seemed to want him there. The question wasn't meant as a dismissal. Why was he suddenly the duke's best friend? "In a moment, Your Grace. I could do with a drink myself. May I bring you one?"

"A brandy for me."

Robbie needed something strong, something to numb his feelings for Heather. But he settled for a glass of champagne. He needed to keep his wits about him, especially now that Stoke was suddenly so chummy with him and his friends. Of course, the man had developed a friendly rapport with Dahlia, which would explain why he was making himself so agreeable to all of them.

But it didn't feel quite right.

Stoke probably sensed something was going on, but he hadn't figured out what it was yet. Or perhaps he had and was working on his own agenda.

Robbie would put his mind to figuring out what Stoke wanted.

After claiming the drinks, he strode onto the veranda in search of his party. Heather was seated on the stone bench beside the balustrade, and the others were standing beside her. "Are ye feeling any better, lass?"

Heather looked up at him, seeming ready to crumble. "Yes, thank you. Much."

No one believed her.

Robbie didn't want Stoke looking at her, so he stepped between them and engaged the duke in conversation. "Did ye know Liverpool was going to call me back?" he asked, not caring for the answer, only that he was distracting the man from looking too closely at Heather.

Och, his pixie.

Her dream was falling apart, and she was trying to hold it together by frayed threads.

Robbie placed the blame squarely on himself. He should have stepped forward and made his feelings known to her from the first. But they'd both tried to take the easy way out instead of fighting for what their hearts wanted...what their hearts needed, and that was each other.

And yet, even acknowledging these feelings, how could their love ever survive? There were problems to be worked out, sacrifices one would have to make for the other. Were they insurmountable? What if they were? He could not bear the thought of leaving Heather brokenhearted.

"I was the one who put your name forward to replace MacDonald.

I'm sorry, lad. I know you wanted to return home, but England needs you to restore calm. He would have destroyed the Scots Greys, you know. There isn't a lord willing to approve the Scottish military budget if MacDonald is behind it. I know the vote won't be until next December, but he is best removed now to give you time to repair the damage he's done."

Robbie nodded. "I'll do what I can."

The wily old man knew his soft spot—the Scots Greys. He'd do anything to protect them. He'd also do anything to protect Heather.

So why had he been such a fool and tried to run from her?

It hadn't been to protect her, but to give them both an easy way of avoiding their feelings for each other.

Stoke patted him on the back. "Good to have you back, MacLauren. Excuse me, but I see Lord Bramble has been trying to catch my eye."

The duke walked off, leaving him with Heather, Dahlia, and Ronan. "Pixie," he said gently.

"No! You ambushed me! Why are you here?" She wasn't frowning at him so much as looking desperately heartbroken.

Now Dahlia was getting overset. "It isn't Robbie's fault. Holly and I made our husbands bring him."

"Why? To purposely destroy my chance at happiness?" She gave none of them time to respond before she rose and darted down the steps into the garden.

"I'll go after her," Robbie said, knowing he was probably the worst person to be seen with her, but he no longer cared. He blamed himself for this mess. After all, he'd read *The Book of Love* and understood the wisdom in the words.

Still, he'd chosen to ignore all its teachings and had purposely put on blinders. Convinced himself to take the easy way out. Lied to himself and Heather. Lied to everyone. Ignored his heart. "Pixie, where are ye?"

He followed the path illuminated by torches to a row of lilac trees now blooming and giving off a fragrant scent that carried on the lightest breeze. There was a stone bench just beyond the lilacs, and he saw her lithe body softly outlined in the amber glow of torchlight.

He made his presence known, not wishing to alarm her, and then sank onto the bench beside her. "Lass, it's time we stopped pretending."

She was in tears.

He could hear her soft sniffles.

His little pixie was miserable and frightened of her feelings. Now that they'd shared a kiss, she could not stop her barricades from tumbling down.

"Robbie, how could you do this to me?" she whispered as he took her in his arms. "Why are you trying to shatter my dreams?"

He was lost to love and could never let her go, but this was not what she wanted to hear. She was trying to continue the pretense, ignore the fact that her girlhood dream was falling apart because she did not love her marquess.

He caressed her cheek, the very one bearing the cut she'd received earlier this morning when the pouch had hit her in the face. *That book. That damn book.* It was going to bedevil them until they faced the truth. "Och, lass. It is no' me doing this to ye."

"Then, who? Just tell me straight out. Who is out to destroy my happiness?"

CHAPTER SEVEN

H EATHER NEVER FELT more miserable in her life.

Even as she tossed the question accusingly at Robbie, she knew the answer. Who was out to destroy her happiness? The blame fell squarely on her. To be precise, she blamed her heart. It wasn't merely leading her to Robbie but tugging at her fiercely. Shoving her at him. Screaming his name. "This cannot be."

It took everything she had in her to resist, and still, it was hopeless. She'd known it the moment she set eyes on his magnificent form in Tilbury's ballroom. He always looked handsome as sin when in his military garb.

She usually saw him in that, for he rarely dressed in civilian clothes. It was so easy to pretend the uniform was what made the butterflies in her stomach come alive.

Yet, here he stood before her, dressed in formal attire and looking resplendent. His black jacket stretched across his broad shoulders and outlined his muscled form. He was hard and lean, big across his chest and shoulders, and trim at his waist. His legs were long and powerfully muscled.

The black of his jacket also accentuated the gold of his hair and the glorious green of his eyes. He looked dashing and elegant, and yet there was a rugged edge to him that stirred her butterflies into a frenzy.

He stood before her like a warrior, exuding power. Strength.

Golden magnificence.

"*Heether*, I did no' wish it to happen either. I wanted ye to have yer dream. No one wishes for yer happiness more than I."

"Then leave me be, Robbie. *Please*. I'm begging you."

"It is no' me ye need to convince, lass. Ye know it is yerself who's causing ye this pain." He tucked his arm around her as she crumbled against him, knowing how wretched she was feeling at this moment.

"How can I trust that you will love me forever, Robbie? How can I trust that you'd be faithful even for a week? You reeked of stale perfume this morning. You'd obviously been with a woman last night, wrapped up in a tawdry affair."

"I dinna touch any woman last night."

"You reeked of–"

"I will no' deny I was in a gaming hell. The sort of establishment where more than mere games of chance take place. Aye, there were women there. I did no' have any of them. I played cards."

"But this is your life, Robbie. Don't you see? Will you expect me to be the sort of wife who stands by meekly and utters not a word while you go off each night to engage in your amusements? I'd never stand for it."

"Nor would I expect ye to. Why ever would ye think I'd behave as I did in my bachelor days?" He could see the doubt in her eyes, and it hurt to know she thought so little of him.

"Are you saying you'd come home to me after work each night?"

"Aye, lass. Upon my oath, I'd be a faithful husband to ye. I'd commit my heart and body to ye, and ye alone. If I were yer husband, I'd have ye fall asleep in my arms each night, and ye'd wake to find me beside ye in the morning."

"Are you saying we would share sleeping quarters?"

"Aye, if ye wished it."

"For how long?"

He tried not to frown, for he'd expected her doubts and knew he was solely to blame for giving rise to them. He'd never been faithful. He'd never been steady. But he'd never been in love before, nor had he ever lied to a woman and let her think she meant more to him than she did. He had never belonged to one woman as he now wished to belong to Heather. "Do ye think I'm the sort of man who would abide ye in my bed only long enough to breed heirs?"

He did not await her answer before continuing. "I dinna want us to have separate lives. If we married, ye'd have my heart. All of it. Ye'd have my body. All of it, too. I'd never betray ye."

His words were only causing her more pain. "I want to believe you, Robbie. I wish I could." She wiped away a few more tears, knowing she needed to stop before her eyes permanently remained that telltale red, and Tilbury would realize she had been crying.

Robbie handed her his handkerchief. "Here, lass."

"Thank you." She dabbed at her eyes. "It isn't fair of you to toss this at me now, Robbie. Not at this last moment. I'm to be married in a matter of days."

"Then why are ye in tears? Why are we out here, both of us miserable and brokenhearted? Ye ran away from reading the book with me, but there is nowhere else for either of us to run, my sweet pixie. We're caught."

"No! I may have avoided reading that book with you. But you *physically* went away. You left me. How can I be sure you won't do it again?"

"It is not at all the same. Ye wanted yer marquess. I was trying to do the right thing by stepping aside."

"You abandoned me, Robbie."

She may as well have slapped him; he felt so insulted. "I backed out like a gentleman to allow ye to pursue yer dream. If not for the damn oath I gave yer sisters, stupidly promising to read the book with ye, I would have stayed away until after the wedding."

"You should have stayed away."

He wanted to shake her until her teeth rattled. Why was she fighting the obvious? "I gave my oath."

"And now this book has placed a curse on us. It will not let you leave."

"It is no' that book holding me in London. Lord Liverpool has commanded me to stay. He's threatened to shoot me if I try to return home to Caithness. He will, too." He sighed and shook his head. "Let me court ye, Heather."

"What!" She obviously wanted to pound her fists against his chest. "Now? With me betrothed to Tilbury and getting married next week? Have you lost all reason?"

"Perhaps. But this is the heart of the matter, isn't it? Are ye going to marry him? Or will ye follow yer heart and marry me?"

"Oh, that's rich. Suddenly I'm to marry you? I'm supposed to believe you want to marry me? That it isn't your sense of competition speaking? Or some terrible spell cast by that wicked book?"

He looked at her aghast. "There's nothing evil about that book."

She curled her hands into fists. "If I broke off my betrothal to Tilbury, would you really step forward and offer for my hand in marriage?"

"Aye."

"Are you certain? Do you not think that once I'm available, the passion will die out of you? What will you do when you find you've suddenly had a change of heart, and I wasn't so precious to you after all?"

"Lass, what are ye talking about? This is no' a game for me."

"I'm *ungettable* now. But if I were to break it off with Tilbury, I'd be just another available female for you to conquer. How long before you tired of me? Don't you see, Robbie? This is why you want me. It's that low brain nature in you, compelling you to conquer and mate."

"Pixie, that's ridiculous. Ye've never been that to me."

"Haven't I? Once you've won me, what then? Robbie, you have

never been a one-woman man. In all these years, has no one ever caught your fancy?" She answered for him. "No, there's been no one. Do you dare deny it?"

"No, lass. I dinna deny it."

"Have you ever courted a woman even for a month?"

"That is no' a fair question. Most of my life has been spent with the Scots Greys. Perhaps not always in wartime, but always on duty. On occasion, quite hazardous duty. I have no' had the luxury of courting."

"But other soldiers in your dragoon regiment have. They've managed to form attachments to their sweethearts. So how am I to believe you would love me and be faithful to me for the rest of our lives when you've never been capable of it before?" She emitted a mirthless laugh. "Well, I've answered my own question, haven't I?"

She sank onto the garden bench. "You told me earlier today that if you ever allowed yourself to fall in love, it would be with me."

"Bollocks," he said with a groan. "*If*...och, lass. It's done. I'm there. My barriers are all down. My heart is in pieces. Pixie, I love ye. I love ye so much, I was willing to let ye go because I thought ye'd be happiest with Tilbury. I'd still let ye go if I thought this. Ye're all that matters to me."

He gazed up at the moon and pointed to it as it stood in full glow against the dark sky, beautiful and silver against the velvet blackness. It was a clear night. Nothing obscured the thousands of gleaming stars.

"I'd hand ye that moon and those stars if ye asked for them," he said, his voice deep and resonant. "I'd find a way to bring them down and put them in the cup of your hands."

She was almost convinced, swept away by the beauty of the night, the light breeze, and delicate scent of lilacs. Swept away by Robbie, by all of him. His look, his subtle musk scent, the exquisite touch of his lips.

His delicious brogue.

Indeed, another moment and she would have gone to Tilbury and just let the feathers fly. But she stilled at the sudden sound of another couple who'd crept to the opposite side of the lilac trees, too lost in each other to even notice her and Robbie seated just on the other side of the arbor barrier.

But this couple was not in love or lost in passion. They were quietly arguing...a tryst breaking up.

Oh, sweet mercy!

How were she and Robbie any different? How long before his roaming eye crushed all hope of love surviving between them?

She threw his handkerchief back at him and ran back to the ballroom.

Dahlia and Holly must have been watching for her. She had no sooner walked back in than they surrounded her and led her straight up to the ladies' retiring room. It was empty for the moment, but others would come up as soon as the dance set ended, so they would not have much time alone.

Dahlia wet her handkerchief and dabbed it against Heather's eyes. "What did you and Robbie say to each other?"

"Why are you both torturing me?" She took the handkerchief from Dahlia's grasp and pressed it to her eyes. "You've meddled enough. It has to end now."

Holly looked bereft. "Then, nothing has changed?"

"Not a blessed thing. I am marrying Tilbury, and I want you to both stop now, or I shall..." She took a deep, agonized breath. "...or I shall never speak to either of you again."

She didn't mean it.

She took it back with her next breath. "No, I'd die if I couldn't spill my heart to you."

They knew she hadn't meant it.

But they also knew they had to end their interference.

"Robbie and I spoke," she said, sounding quite miserable, which she was. "We heard each other out. We came to the same conclusion we reach every time we confront our feelings for each other. We simply are not meant to be."

"But you do have feelings for him?" Holly asked, seeming to have great difficulty taking this in.

"You married twice, Holly. You found love a second time around. This proves we can love more than one person in our lifetime."

Holly's response, one that Heather knew was not going to be one of agreement, was cut short as other ladies came in.

She and her sisters left to return to the ballroom.

They were about to walk in, when out of the corner of her eye, she noticed Robbie standing beside a decorative niche. His arms were crossed over his chest, and he was looking at her; no doubt he'd waited for her and wanted to continue their conversation.

For this reason, he did not notice the beautiful woman who came up behind him and touched him as though they were intimate friends. Heather felt ill, watching this likely former paramour gain his attention by rubbing herself against his arm.

Robbie appeared startled, but he allowed this woman to draw him into the niche. It wasn't for very long, hardly long enough for a kiss.

But it was enough for Heather.

He stepped back out and took one look at her.

He knew she'd seen the exchange.

To her surprise, she felt his sorrow as a tangible thing radiating from his heart. It surrounded her and shook her as though his sadness was reaching out, desperate for her understanding and forgiveness.

Could he feel her sorrow?

She entered the ballroom, needing to be away from him.

Tilbury smiled at her as she and her sisters joined him. He was still standing with the Duke of Stoke and Lady Melinda, the three of them laughing over some childhood exploit Tilbury and Melinda had shared. Their families had been good friends for ages and often spent time with each other at their country homes. He smiled at her, a genuinely warm smile. "There you are, my dear. I hoped you would show up to rescue me."

She returned his smile. "You do not appear to need rescuing."

"Oh, but I do. Melly was reminding me of the frog she put in my boot when we were children, and how I cried and ran off to tattle on her to the adults. Not my proudest moment, I will admit."

"He still detests frogs," Melinda said in a mock whisper meant to be heard by all of them in their small party. "Which is why I call him Toad whenever I wish to tease him."

Dahlia shot her a look.

She knew what it was about. Tilbury had referred to Lady Melinda as Melly. She had playfully called him Toad.

Heather frowned back at her sister. It was no different than Robbie always referring to her as his pixie. Of course, Robbie was now claiming to be in love with her. Tilbury was doing no such thing with Lady Melinda.

Tilbury held out his hand. "Heather, we haven't danced since we opened the ball. I'm sure I owe you another."

It was another waltz.

"Yes, of course." She briefly wondered whether Robbie would ask that beautiful woman who had accosted him a few minutes ago to dance with him.

No, she had to stop thinking of him.

What he did no longer mattered.

But she could not stop looking for him out of the corner of her eye. She cringed when she saw the woman twirl past her in the arms of...no, it wasn't Robbie. Thank goodness. Although, why should she care?

"Heather, you seem distracted," Tilbury said. "Am I no longer fascinating company?"

She shook her head. "Do forgive me. This ball is beautiful and rather overwhelming. All eyes are on me now that I am to be your marchioness. I don't want to disappoint you."

He cast her another pleasant smile. "You're doing fine. Don't worry what others think of you. Just be yourself, and they will love you."

As you do?

She didn't have the spine to ask him.

In truth, she feared the answer. He'd never once said he loved her. He'd merely offered to marry her. She had naturally assumed love was the reason.

He twirled her in his arms, following the circular path of dancers at a leisurely pace. "You did not seem pleased to see Captain MacLauren this evening."

The comment caused her to miss a step, but she quickly recovered. "It wasn't displeasure, merely surprise. He intended to leave for Scotland today. He told us he would not be attending this ball. He was quite certain about it." By *us*, she meant *me*, but it seemed safest not to single herself out.

"I suppose Stoke and I are to blame for that. We've been pressuring Lord Liverpool to remove the current Scottish liaison to Parliament. The man's an insufferable blowhard and a disgrace to the proud Scottish regiments. I don't know how we exercised such poor judgment in confirming him in the first place. But the moment Captain MacLauren returned, we knew we had to make him stay."

Heather began to nibble her lip.

What an odd and dismaying turn of events. Her betrothed was the very man who was behind Robbie's remaining in London and further tormenting her heart.

Tilbury continued his glowing assessment of Robbie. "He's a very good man. Smart. Diligent. If he gives you his oath, he keeps to it."

Why was he telling her this?

She nodded. "My brothers-in-law think highly of him as well."

"And what do you think of him, Heather? You always seem to frown at him whenever he is in your company. Has he said something to you? Or behaved in an ungentlemanly fashion toward you? I know he is a hound, but I've never heard of him treating respectable ladies—"

"No, he's always been a perfect gentleman around me." Her heart shot into her throat. "I don't frown at him. Why should I? Why are we even talking about him? Should we not be talking about our upcoming wedding? Or the rest of our lives together?"

He shrugged as they glided across the floor, still in time with the other dancers. "Aren't all the arrangements in order? Have you packed your belongings?"

"Not yet, but I will have it done in plenty of time. I don't have all that much, just my gowns and their accessories."

"I'll arrange to have them brought over to my residence while we're at the church. The most we have left to do is remember to show up at St. Mary's on the morning of our wedding day."

"Remember to show up?" She laughed a little too eagerly, her inane, twittering trill sounding shrill even to her own ears. "Why would either of us forget?"

"We wouldn't, my dear." He drew her a little closer, almost as though comforting her. It wasn't a passionate gesture. In truth, it felt like a consoling gesture. "Heather, would you mind terribly if we cut short the dance? I see someone I've needed to speak to tonight, and he is now standing alone."

"If you must. Of course, I don't mind."

"Very gracious of you, my dear. Let me find you a suitable partner. I don't want to leave you in the lurch."

"No, it's all right. Don't worry about me. I'll return to my sisters until—"

"Ah, here's someone."

Heather almost fainted when they twirled past Robbie, and Tilbury suddenly called him over. "Captain MacLauren, might I impose on you?"

Robbie eyed them both warily.

"You see, I must speak to Lord Wembley. It is terribly rude of me to abandon my betrothed. Would you please finish the dance with her?"

Robbie nodded, but cast her a *what-the-hell* glance the moment they were left on their own. "*Heether,*" he said, his brogue pronounced and a mark of his concern, "what in blazes did ye say to him?"

"Nothing, I promise. Oh, Robbie. This whole evening feels wrong."

"I've upset ye, lass." He took her in his arms and began to lead her expertly along to the tune of the music and the flow of the other dancers. There was nothing improper in the way he held her, but there didn't have to be. She was in his arms, and this was enough to make her come alive.

"No, it isn't only you."

He was big and handsome, and his touch had her skin tingling.

Candlelight shone on his golden hair so that it took on a rich, amber hue. She never tired of looking at his handsome face or in the dangerous emerald pools of his eyes. She ached so badly to remain in his arms forever.

Oh, how she longed to be held and loved by this powerful man.

Why would this feeling not go away?

"Robbie, why would he contrive to have me dance with you? I feel like everything is spinning out of control, and I can do nothing to stop it."

"I dinna know, lass. Perhaps he senses my feelings for ye and wishes to test us. Rather, test you. He could no' give a rat's arse for my feelings." He gave her hand a light squeeze. "I won't interfere between the two of ye. I've laid my heart bare to ye, and it is now up to ye to come to me willingly or no'. I'll love ye and protect ye no matter what ye decide."

"Don't say that, Robbie. You're going to make me cry. Who was that woman who approached you earlier?"

He clenched his jaw. "No one important."

"She thought she was. Perhaps not now to you, but at one time."

His eyes took on a hard glint. "Never. Pixie, ye live in yer sheltered world and think people are well-intentioned. They're no'. I was never more to her than a quick...she's married. She detests her husband, and I suspect by now the feeling is mutual. She married the baron for his wealth and title. I could get crude, but I will no' with ye."

He shook his head and sighed. "She never meant anything to me, nor do I believe I hold any particular tenderness in her heart. I am no' proud of my behavior in the past, but I will own up to it. I canno' take it back. However, this is no longer who I am."

She cast him a guilty look.

"Och, ye think I am faithless and will easily be led astray. If ye think that, then ye're wrong. There is nothing beautiful about a woman who would break her vows to her husband."

"But Robbie, I kissed you. I am betrothed to Tilbury, and I kissed you. Did I not break a vow?"

"Pixie, no. What ye gave me with that kiss was yer heart. Everything ye do, the tears ye shed, the fretting ye do, and the ache ye feel, are because ye are struggling to understand what yer precious heart wants. What it needs. Ye dinna use people. Ye try never to hurt people."

"But I'm hurting everyone, aren't I?"

"Not intentionally. And ye're hurting yerself worst." He frowned as the dance drew to an end. "I wish ye trusted me. I wish ye believed I could be faithful to ye." Another woman tossed him a look as he held out his arm to escort Heather back to Tilbury's side.

She saw it.

He saw it, too.

"My past coming back to haunt me. So be it, lass. I dinna fault ye for not trusting me. But I give ye my oath, if I were yer husband, I'd never give ye a moment's doubt about me."

When they reached their small party, he gave a polite bow and took himself off.

Heather wanted so badly to believe him. "Oh, excuse me," she said to Tilbury and Lord Wembly. "I think I left my fan upstairs in the ladies' retiring room."

She followed after Robbie.

He had not taken two steps out the ballroom doors when another female accosted him.

Heather closed her eyes as a wave of pain shot through her. Even though Robbie shook off this woman as well, there would come a day when he would once again accept these invitations.

She had to admit it to herself.

She'd made the right choice in Tilbury.

And yet, why did it feel so wrong?

CHAPTER EIGHT

V IOLET GAVE BIRTH on the night of the ball, and to everyone's
surprise, Romulus made it home with his young cabin boy,
Innes Buchan, the Duke of Buchan's nine-year-old son, minutes before
their daughter was born.

The two of them were heard stomping in shortly before dawn,
exhausted and dusty but delighted to be home.

Heather was still awake and hurried downstairs when she heard
the butler open the door to allow them in. Romulus had looked up at
her on the steps, worry furrowing his brow. "How's Violet?"

"She's in labor. Uncle George is stretched out on the sofa in your
library. The midwife is upstairs with her. All appears to be progressing
as it ought to be."

She could tell by the bob of his Adam's apple that his heart was in
his throat. "I have to see her."

Heather nodded. "Do go up. She'll be happy to see you. But don't
get too close. You have to wash the dirt off you first. Innes, come with
me. I'll show you to your room and help you get settled. How was
your trip?"

The boy groaned. "We rode until our horses were ready to drop.
Captain Brayden fretted the whole way. Is Mrs. Brayden...Violet...all
right?"

"Yes, she's holding up. Still trying to get the baby out, but Uncle
George and the midwife saw no cause for worry. The baby will arrive

soon."

They had just dropped Innes's pouch in his guest chamber when they heard a high-pitched wail.

Heather gasped, her earlier turmoil over Robbie momentarily forgotten as they celebrated the arrival of this newborn Brayden. A baby girl they called Hyacinth.

She thought it was very sweet the way Innes marveled over Romulus and Violet's new daughter, repeating her name as though she could understand he was calling to her. The lad spent hours standing over the cradle, watching her little prune face wrinkle and her rosebud lips twitch whenever she was ready to suckle. "She's so tiny and delicate."

Romulus, of course, was beaming. No one could wipe the grin off his face or the love in his eyes for the two women now in his life. He would not leave Violet's side other than to peer into the cradle where his daughter was swaddled and sleeping. "What do you think, Innes? Isn't Hyacinth a beauty?"

The boy nodded. "The most beautiful sight in the world."

Heather had been staying with Violet while Romulus was away and remained with them mostly to keep Innes company. This allowed Violet and Romulus to have some time alone, although with family traipsing through the house to celebrate the new arrival, they did not have all that much time to themselves.

In any event, Innes was there and in need of some attention. Heather took it upon herself to look after him. She asked about his trip and told him all about the grand ball Tilbury had thrown.

"Was my father there?" Innes asked, his gaze so hopeful, she felt a pang to her heart for the sadness of it.

"Yes, but I did not have the chance to speak to him." She patted the boy's hand. "I'm sure Romulus will send word to him tomorrow. He's a little distracted today."

Innes nodded. "It doesn't matter. My father's wife will make up some excuse about why he cannot see me. She always does."

"Oh, Innes. I'm so sorry." She did not know what to say to cheer this lonely boy. "Well, Harry and Charles were asking after you the other day. They'll be delighted to know you've come home. Harry has some new marbles he's eager to show you."

That cheered the boy a little.

Two days after Romulus and Innes arrived, Heather was assigned the task of taking Innes to meet his father. The subterfuge necessary for father and son to steal a few hours together angered her. For pity's sake, the man was a duke. Could he not put his witch of a wife in her place and tell her the boy was important to him?

But it was at this clandestine meeting of father and son, held at Ronan's office in the Parliament building, that she caught sight of Robbie again. Of course, his office had always been next door to Ronan's. She did not know why she'd thought it would have moved. And now that he was back in the role of Scottish military liaison to Parliament, there he was, clad in his uniform and looking as splendid as ever.

He'd seen her standing in the hall, just outside of Ronan's office. "Pixie, I dinna expect to find ye here. Are ye waiting for Ronan?"

"No." She pointed to the closed door. "I brought Innes Buchan to see his father."

"Och, the poor lad." Robbie nodded, knowing the full story. "Where's Ronan?"

"He was called to a meeting downstairs with Lord Liverpool and the Lord Admiral. Something about the *Invictus* debacle last winter. Lord Peckham is fighting to restore his brother to the command of the vessel." She rolled her eyes. "How can he be so ignorant and pompous? His brother, Viscount Hawley, was the fool who ran the ship aground. A fleet flagship, no less. The man's an idiot, and they made him a fleet admiral?"

Robbie nodded. "This is how it is, lass. These lords think the privilege of their birth gives them the right to anything they want. This is why I hate this assignment, having to deal with louts like Peckham and Hawley. I just want to kick their arses into the Thames."

Heather grinned. "I would be cheering you on. Ronan almost died trying to get that warship back into deep waters. And Lord Peckham had the gall to try to make Ronan out to be the goat when everyone with half a brain knew he was the hero in that fiasco."

"Dinna get worked up. It's done and over. Ronan and the Lord Admiral are merely tying up loose ends. Hawley will never get command of so much as a child's toy boat again. Peckham has quietly been retired from the Admiralty. Not quite the punishment they deserved, but it's something." He held out his arm to her. "Care to take a stroll along the Thames? We won't be long. Just a quick turn. I'll bring ye back well before the lad's visit is over. Besides, Innes knows to wait in Ronan's office if the reunion with his father ends earlier than expected."

She nodded. "All right. I'd like that."

He cast her an affectionate smile as he led her downstairs and onto the promenade alongside the river. The sun warmed her shoulders, and the light breeze off the water felt refreshing. "I hear Violet had a little girl. Romulus must be popping his buttons, his chest puffed out with pride. Will ye let them know I send my best wishes?"

"Yes." She shook her head and laughed. "He is walking on air. I don't think his feet have touched the ground since his daughter wailed to announce her arrival into the world. She already has her papa wrapped around her little finger."

Now that they were on the promenade, he walked with his hands clasped behind his back, strolling beside her, but they were no longer touching. "And how is Violet?"

"Doing very well. She's also on a cloud, so happy to have Romulus home." They walked in silence for a few moments, thoroughly enjoying the sun and the breeze sweeping off the water. The sun shone on Robbie's hair, giving it that golden sun god aura. He truly was the handsomest man she'd ever set eyes upon. His features were rugged and masculine, not at all soft or styled.

His eyes, however, were what melted her heart and also caused her the greatest pain. They were sharp and assessing, but so gentle whenever he fixed his gaze upon her. "Robbie, they are so much in love."

She caught the flicker of anguish in his expression. "I know, lass. How are yer wedding plans coming along?"

She swallowed hard. "All in order. Please, let's not talk about Tilbury and me, or else I'll cry."

He lifted her hand and covered it with his own. "Och, my little pixie. Ye know this is not how it should be."

"I know. My mind should be on him, and I should be joyful. This is my dream coming true, yet now it feels…"

"How is he treating ye?"

"Courteously, as ever." She did not have to tell him there was still no passion between them. Her expression revealed it all.

A troubled look crept in his eyes, but he said nothing more about it.

"What are you thinking, Robbie?"

He shook his head. "Nothing, it is something too farfetched to consider."

"What?"

"I'll let ye know if it's something other than a foolish thought. I'd tell ye if it was anything to concern ye, lass. Let's just enjoy the walk."

"All right." She wanted to ask him if he would attend her wedding, but it was simply too cruel to ask this of him. He had been invited. She would understand if he chose not to attend. "We ought to turn back now."

"Aye, lass."

"Robbie, the family comes by every day to see Romulus, Violet, and the baby. Being part Farthingale, they had to give her a flower name, too. Hyacinth."

He grinned. "Of course. It's a pretty name."

"I think she will have Violet's dark hair and violet eyes. Her hair is little more than dark tufts right now. It's hard to tell whether her eyes will remain violet. We won't know for certain for another month or two."

They resumed walking, but Robbie still kept hold of her hand, now having tucked it once more in the crook of his elbow. She liked his touch, found it solid and comforting.

She liked being by his side and was amazed by how perfectly they seemed to fit together. It was odd. He was big and brawny. She was fine-boned and, while not small, not all that big either. Yet, it felt as though they were made for each other.

At times like these, she could imagine herself married to this man and being happy. But the women who had approached him at the ball were still vivid in her mind.

She could not readily forget them.

Well, not them...what she could not get over were her own doubts.

And yet, she trusted him.

Perhaps it was these women she did not trust, for they would not care about Robbie's marital status when seeking his attention.

In truth, it was herself she doubted. She had yet to figure out what she had to offer an accomplished man like Robbie. But if she followed that thought, then what interest could Tilbury possibly have in her?

She stifled a shudder, no longer knowing what to think or feel. Robbie believed he loved her. She did not doubt that he felt it sincerely. Tilbury had never once said he loved her. So why did he wish to marry her?

She knew she ought to confront Tilbury and ask him this and oth-er hard questions. Indeed, she had to do it before they exchanged vows, or then it would be too late to back out if she did not like his answers.

She'd been a ninny not to question him beforehand.

The blame fell squarely on her shoulders. She had been so caught up in the idea of becoming a marchioness, she hadn't bothered to probe deeper, and now it was going to plague her until she learned the answers.

First and foremost, why did Tilbury wish to marry her?

"Pixie, yer thoughts seem to be drifting out to sea along with the current," Robbie said, easing her back to the present.

She shook her head. "Yes, my head is full to bursting. But I'm enjoying my time with you."

"The feeling is mutual, lass. I'm always at ease in yer company, but ye know this."

"As I am always at ease in yours. I wonder why, Robbie. We are so different, and yet I won't deny that we have a strong connection. How does *The Book of Love* explain it? We should be strangers, and yet I feel as though you know me better than I know myself."

"I dinna have the answer for ye. I thought it was just the five senses working their magic, but it is more than just liking the look of ye or the scent of yer body. And aye, what would a Highlander have in common with a Sassenach city girl? Yet we do have a bond between us, as though our hearts are woven together. I can only speak for mine. Ye fill it with happiness. I dinna know why. Ye just do."

She gave his arm a little squeeze, knowing she would cry if she shared her deepest feelings. He knew it anyway. She was terrible at hiding anything, and he saw straight into her heart. "My parents will be arriving tomorrow. They'll stay with Holly and Joshua."

"Will ye move in there, too?"

"No, I'll remain with Violet and Romulus. I'm sure Uncle John and Aunt Sophie will have everyone over soon, an informal family gathering to welcome my parents to London. The MacLaurens count as family. Consider yourself invited."

"Thank ye, lass."

"And you are welcome to stop in at Violet's whenever you wish," she said, returning the conversation to her cousin's new baby. "Violet's sister, Poppy, and her husband, Nathaniel, will arrive soon. They had planned to come to town for my…" What was wrong with her? She could not bring herself to call it her wedding. "Anyway, I believe you know them."

"I do, lass. I was at Sherbourne Manor when my cousin, Thad, made an arse of himself over Nathaniel's sister, Penelope. That is also where my brother met his wife."

"Yes, the Earl of Wycke's sister. He's family now that he married my cousin, Honey."

Robbie let out a throaty chuckle. "I think yer family is connected to everyone in London."

She nodded. "We are a large clan."

They paused beside the river for several minutes, watching the boats and barges sail by. Robbie's gaze remained mainly on her, studying her. Soaking her in. Finally, he leaned his elbows against the fence separating the Parliament promenade from the river, turning his back to the river to face her. "Pixie, I will no' deny that I was a hound in my younger days. I've never denied it or made excuses to ye about it. I know I was one of the worst, and I've told ye so. But I am not that man any longer. My past still follows me, as ye saw at Tilbury's ball, and I canno' change that. But it is the past. It is no longer me."

She nodded but stayed silent to hear him out.

"These women have no' changed, but I have. I hope for the better. I wish to be someone worthy of ye."

His words were like daggers piercing her fragile soul.

"I'm no' asking ye to accept me. But I want ye to know, ye put magic in my heart. If ye truly love Tilbury, then he should be putting magic in yer heart. What concerns me is that I see no sign of it from either of ye. Yer wedding is only a few days away, and I've never seen two people more unengaged. This ought to be one of the happiest and most important events of yer life."

"I know," she said in a broken whisper.

"My sweet lass, I'm worried about ye. I've never seen a more miserable bride."

She wasn't angry with him.

He'd spoken nothing but the truth.

"Robbie, please. Don't you think my stomach has been in knots over this? I haven't even seen Tilbury since the ball. I don't know what we're doing, he and I. In truth, I feel so lost."

He took her hand again. "Ye have only to turn to me. I'll always protect ye. Whatever ye wish to do, I'll stand beside ye."

They returned upstairs just as the Duke of Buchan was finishing his visit with his son. "It was good to see you, Innes. I love you, my son." He hugged the boy.

The boy hugged him back fiercely. "I miss you, Papa. I want to come home."

The duke's eyes misted. "It's best not yet. Soon, though."

Robbie tucked an arm around Heather's shoulder when he sensed she was going to cry as well. He knew her so well. Indeed, she felt her eyes misting. It was so unfair. How could the duke allow his jealous wife to destroy his special relationship with his son?

"You be a good lad. Listen to what Captain Brayden tells you."

"I do, Papa. He's very smart, and he never makes a mistake."

He ruffled the boy's blond curls. "Does he treat you kindly?"

The boy nodded. "And he let me hold his new baby daughter. She's the size of a potato, she's that small. Her name is Hyacinth."

His father smiled down at him. "Hyacinth? What a pretty name."

Innes shook his head again. "She's beautiful. But she's still very wrinkled."

The boy was unbearably sad once his father departed, so Robbie suggested they sneak into Lord Liverpool's private dining room and appropriate some scones.

Innes looked up at Robbie with big, earnest eyes. "Appropriate? Is that the same as stealing?"

Heather tried to hold back her laughter, which ended in an unlady-like snort.

Robbie was grinning again, casting his charm over them. "Och, no. We are taking possession of them for an important use...to feed our hungry bellies. This is the way Parliament works. We take things for the better good. I take from you. You take from me. We both take from someone else."

Innes nodded. "Stealing."

Heather burst out laughing. "You are right, Innes. But in this situation, Lord Liverpool keeps his dining room stocked so that members can help themselves to a light refreshment should they feel the need. He allows it, so it isn't quite the same."

The rest of the afternoon passed pleasantly, and she was sorry when they had to depart. Robbie said nothing more to her about her upcoming wedding.

He did not need to. She knew what had to be done. All she had lacked before was the courage to confront Tilbury and have a serious discussion with him. In her defense, she had not realized how wrong it all was until Robbie had returned and turned her heart inside out. But she had to be true to herself and needed to ask the hard questions.

She wrote to Tilbury as soon as she returned home. "Romulus, may I ask one of your footmen to deliver this note?"

"Yes, of course. I'll have Rollins take it over right away. Should he wait for a response?"

She hadn't thought of that. "Yes, if Tilbury is at home. Otherwise, he can just leave it for him. I'm sure he'll send word to me once he sees it."

But the day passed without any return correspondence or news from him. When she heard nothing from him the next day, she assumed he must have been unexpectedly called out of town since no one had seen him in the halls of Parliament or at the various social affairs. Still, shouldn't he have dropped her a note, no matter how brief?

She thought little of it since her parents had now arrived, and her attention turned to them. She hurried over to Holly's home to greet them. "Mama! Papa! How was your trip down?"

"Smooth, for the most part," her father said, giving her a warm embrace.

"But we did hit a ghastly patch of rain just north of Grantham." Her mother also greeted her affectionately, kissing her on the cheek and smiling broadly. "My little marchioness! It's so good to see you. It's so good to see all of my daughters again."

Heather rolled her eyes. "Mama, I'm not a marchioness yet."

"Oh, piffle. The wedding is almost upon us. I may as well get used to referring to you as Lady Tilbury."

Dahlia had come by as well, and Holly had set out tea and light refreshments for them as they sat in the parlor and caught up on all that was happening.

Once they'd caught up on the mundane topics, the weather, the coaching inns, the sights, and shopping they would take in while in London, the conversation turned to Heather's wedding. "When shall we meet your marquess?" her mother asked, reaching out to give her hand a light squeeze. "Is he handsome? Is he rich?"

"Mama! What a question to ask. I'm not marrying him for his wealth or title." Although this was not entirely true. Tilbury was a very pleasant fellow, and she liked him, but she had accepted to marry him precisely because he was a marquess. She hadn't bothered to properly consider his offer because she'd always dreamed of being a marchioness.

Of course, if he had been cruel or a boor, she would have refused him. Oddly, had he been a duke or an earl, she would have given the proposal more scrutiny because her heart had never been set on becoming a duchess or countess.

"Heather, dear. Tell us about the wedding plans. Your sisters rushed into marriage so quickly. Military men. Too bad they are merely captains, but I understand they come from a good family and are accepted in the best circles." She paused to frown lightly at Holly and Dahlia. "John and Rupert had full authority to act on our behalf, so I'm sure they ensured you are well protected no matter what happens in your marriages. Too bad their brother, who is an earl, was already taken. And I'm told your cousin, Belle, snared the rich brother, Finn."

Heather exchanged a look with her sisters. "Mama, they've married wonderful men, and these are love matches. Those are the best of all. I'm sure you've met Joshua already. Isn't he wonderful? Have you met his brother, Ronan? I'm very proud to have them in the family."

Dahlia nodded enthusiastically. "We've all been invited to Uncle John's this evening, and you'll have the chance to meet all the Braydens as well as catch up with our family. Ronan will stop by Chipping Way after his duties at Parliament."

"Same for Joshua," Holly said, the nibble of her lip revealing she was fretting. "They'll probably ride over together because they both work in the Parliament buildings."

Her father did not look pleased. "Ah, they are not gentlemen then?"

Heather wanted to reach over and hug both her sisters. It suddenly struck her with such clarity just how above themselves her parents had become. Perhaps they had always been this way, and she'd just been too naive to notice. "They are the best sort of men, Papa. Why are you going on as though we are something above them? I would much rather marry a man who is hardworking and not an indolent dolt."

Her father took a sip of his tea and then set down his cup before responding to her. "I expect they are outstanding men. I don't mean to disparage them. But I have three strikingly beautiful daughters, and I would have thought all three of you would have caught the eye of a peer. Only you have managed it, Heather."

Her mother nodded. "As we always knew you would. A marquess! How clever you are."

Heather now felt ill.

Her stomach was in a roil, and she wanted to cast up her accounts. This is how they had been raised, to marry into a title. Holly's life almost ruined because she'd been pushed to marry into one of York's most prominent families at the tender age of seventeen and found herself a widow at nineteen. Dahlia was publicly humiliated by the lord she thought was courting her only to learn he'd been secretly courting the daughter of an earl all along.

This is why her own foolish dream to marry a marquess had been indulged, nurtured, praised, and heartily encouraged.

Dear heaven! It was a miracle her two sisters had the presence of mind to appreciate the worth of their husbands and fall in love with them even though they were mere captains. "Joshua and Ronan also work with Captain Robert MacLauren. He's the Scottish military liaison to Parliament. You'll meet him this evening at Uncle John's house."

Her parents stared at her in confusion, her father finally speaking up. "And why should we care to meet this captain? And a Scot, no less?"

Her mother nodded. "Shouldn't you be introducing us to the man you're going to marry?"

CHAPTER NINE

"WHERE IS YOUR marquess?" Heather's father asked as he had done several times throughout the day. The family had gathered at Number Three Chipping Way, the home of John and Sophie Farthingale, for a light supper and casual entertainment that evening. The house was packed since all their cousins, and their husbands were there, some bringing their children who were now running through the house, too excited to be playing together to settle down.

Heather had made a point of bringing young Innes over with them, and he was now quietly playing marbles with the older Farthingale boys, Harry and Charles, in her uncle's library.

"I'm sorry, Papa. But Tilbury won't be able to make it tonight."

Instead of frowning, her father seemed pleased. "Of course, he's a very busy man. Must be meeting with all sorts of important people."

She nodded. "Yes, often with Lord Liverpool himself. But Joshua and Ronan are also quite friendly with Liverpool."

"Heather, dear. It isn't the same. They have business dealings with him. But your marquess dines with him socially."

Was it criminal to strangle one's parents?

Perhaps Dahlia and Holly would aid and abet her.

She could see by their expressions that they'd had quite enough of their airs.

They hadn't let up for a moment, not even when they'd stopped next door to visit Violet, Romulus, and their new baby. "Another captain," her mother had whispered in Heather's ear as they'd walked out. "Too bad she was too late to snag his brother. I hear he's the Earl of Exmoor. But Violet seems happy enough with the younger brother. Why must you stay with Violet now that her husband has returned from the sea? Could you not contrive to stay with Exmoor? Or move in with Honey now that she is married to the Earl of Wycke?"

"Mama, stop. They are all excellent men."

"I'm sure they are, my dear."

Ugh. If that did not sound condescending!

And now they were about to sit to supper, and Heather's cheeks were in flames as her parents paid particular attention to the earls present, Exmoor, Westcliff, and Wycke, and ignored the men their daughters had married.

Their behavior was beyond condescending when introduced to Robbie.

"I'm so sorry," she said, remaining beside him once her parents had moved away to greet other members of the family.

"Dinna fash, lass. I've been treated worse." He cast her an endearing grin. "Even by my own family, especially my brother, Malcolm."

She glanced at him in surprise. "I thought you always got along?"

"Aye, we did. But I was the little brother, always challenging him. He'd flick me off him and sometimes give me a kick in the arse to remind me he was bigger and stronger."

Heather giggled. "But you were scrappy."

"That's a polite way of putting it. I was stupid." He glanced at her parents, who were now engaged in conversation with Joshua and Ronan's mother, Lady Miranda. "They only want what's best for ye."

"No, Robbie. They are thinking of their hopes and wishes for me, not my desires for myself. They have no clue what I want."

"Most parents believe they know what's best for their children. Often they do, for they've had more experience and understand how harsh life can sometimes be. They want ye to marry the marquess not merely for the title, but for what it represents. Safety, security. Protection."

"Now you are spouting *The Book of Love* to me." But she wasn't really irritated. How could she be when all she wanted to do was throw her arms around Robbie and hold onto him so tightly, she'd steal the breath from him?

"Aye, lass. That need to survive is built into all of us. It is only natural that yer parents want ye wedded to a powerful man."

She did not wish to leave Robbie's side, so she made a point of sitting beside him as they had their supper. Of course, on more formal occasions, there would be seating arrangements, and the earls would be of foremost prominence at the table. But at the more private family meals, everyone was equal and sat wherever they desired.

The food was set up along two massive buffets, and everyone would serve themselves. Footmen were present to assist but not to serve. Heather smiled at Robbie as they made their way along the queue. Each dish looked appealing. Quail in an apricot glaze and sprinkled with sultanas. Smoked fish. A loin of pork. Mutton stewed in a sweet, port wine. Roasted potatoes and creamed leeks.

"What would ye like, Pixie?"

"Mutton, please. It looks divine." She breathed it in. "There's the sweet wine, of course. But also traces of garlic, and that aroma of mint comes from marjoram. What will you have, Robbie?"

He chuckled. "All of it. As much as will fit on my plate."

Robbie served her and then took a hefty portion for himself.

A footman came around to pour wine in their glasses as soon as they'd settled beside each other. "Ye seem to know a little about cooking. Did ye supervise the kitchen staff at yer home?"

Since the table was crowded, they were huddled close in order to squeeze in all the adults. The children were given over to their governesses and sent to the informal dining area off the kitchen to eat their meals.

Heather was quite content with her seating arrangement, liking the way their bodies touched because Robbie's shoulders were too broad to fit within his confined space. His leg brushed up against hers as well, not on purpose, but simply because they were in too close quarters to avoid it.

"Our staff consisted of one cook who lived in and made our meals. My sisters and I often helped out. I'm a capable cook, but it must be kept a secret. Proper young ladies are not supposed to know their way around a kitchen."

"Lass, ye should have told me sooner. I would have stolen ye away and carried ye off to Gretna Green. Who needs a lass who knows how to dance or properly wave a damn fan? Can ye bake?"

She nodded.

"Now I know I'm in love with ye." He cast her a wink, and she laughed in response. She knew he was making a jest, but there was truth to the remark.

Her parents noticed their conversation and the way they were looking at each other. They frowned at her from across the dining table.

She ignored them and tried to distract Robbie so that he could not see their faces.

Of course, he was too clever to ever be fooled. "Pixie, ye dinna have to protect me," he said, casting her an achingly gentle smile.

"They are behaving abominably. No better than Lord Wainscott when he humiliated Dahlia. I won't allow it, Robbie. I know you are too polite to say anything to them. But I am their daughter. They cannot avoid me. I will not have them insulting my friends."

He arched an eyebrow. "Are we friends now?"

She wanted them to be so much more, but how could she say anything before she'd had the chance to speak to Tilbury? "Yes, friends. I will always carry you in my heart."

Her hand was resting on her lap, and he took it now to discreetly wrap it in his under the table. "Aye, Pixie. Always."

He released her after a moment, and although it had been but a brief touch, she already missed the enveloping warmth of his sure and comforting grip.

Heather was relieved when the evening came to an end. Her parents had made plans with her cousin, Dillie, to be taken on a tour of London. Since Dillie was married to the Duke of Edgeware, her parents would be driven about town in their ducal carriage.

That in itself was a treat worth a trip to London even if they did not manage to visit a single museum or browse in any of the elite ladies' shops on Regent Street or the men's shops on Oxford Street.

Robbie quirked an eyebrow as their plans were organized.

Heather winced back at him, ashamed her parents were effete snobs. All her mother could talk about was tomorrow's excursion and to be seen riding in the park in the Duke of Edgeware's elegant landau.

She had the workings of a pounding headache by the time her parents were saying their farewells. She felt sorry for Holly and Joshua, who would have to endure their chatter for the remainder of the evening, always reminded that neither Holly nor Dahlia had managed to marry a peer.

Robbie walked her and Innes next door.

Innes hurried inside, eager to tell Romulus about the new marble, a green ghost, he'd won from Charles.

Robbie turned to leave, but Heather placed a hand on his arm to halt him. "Will you not come in a moment? I'm sure Romulus is still awake and would not mind sharing a drink with you."

"Pixie, no. I'd best be on my way. But it was nice to share the evening with ye."

She rolled her eyes. "You are only saying this to be polite."

He chuckled. "No, I did enjoy my time with ye...even if it was a little noisy."

MEARA PLATT

"And offensive," she said with a sigh. "Truly, I never realized my parents were such snobs."

"They'll settle down in a day or two. Ye could see they were decent people when they forgot to be insufferable. They wanted the best for their daughters."

She nodded. "Dahlia and Holly did find the best."

"And you?" He was studying her now, awaiting her answer.

"I've sent word to Tilbury, asking to see him. But he hasn't responded to any of my missives. Robbie, it all feels so wrong suddenly. But I don't want to discuss it now."

He caressed her cheek. "Call on me whenever ye're ready to talk. I'll no' be going anywhere for at least another month."

She wanted to throw her arms around him and hold on to him forever but dared not. Even she felt it was too much to do so while about to marry another within a matter of days. She stood in the doorway until Robbie strolled out the front gate. He would collect his horse from the mews at the rear of the house and ride home.

She went inside once he had disappeared from view, her heart in a tight twist, as though someone had wrapped a beefy hand around it and was squeezing the fragile organ with all his might.

She looked in on Innes, kissed him goodnight, and wished him sweet dreams, then retired to her bedchamber and slowly undressed.

She feared sleep would elude her, for her situation with Tilbury was weighing on her mind. Indeed, she slept poorly and awoke early. Since the kitchen staff was awake and already preparing the meals for the day, she took a cup of cocoa and walked outside to the garden.

The bench Robbie had cracked to pieces had been replaced, so she sat in the peaceful quiet, not minding the dampness to the air or the morning chill.

It was now the third day of not hearing from Tilbury, and she was growing concerned. She decided to go along with Dahlia to see the progress of her work at the Duke of Stoke's house and hopefully have

102

a chance to mention his absence to the duke.

After all, they seemed to be quite friendly.

It would not be a long visit, but she needed to take her mind off Tilbury's inexplicable silence. Dahlia was only stopping in to make certain the workmen had delivered the correct wallpaper that would go up tomorrow. "Let's stop at Blakney's pie shop once we're done," Dahlia suggested.

Heather readily agreed.

When they arrived at the duke's home, Heather was shocked to find Tilbury casually having tea with Stoke and Lady Melinda.

He rose at once. "My dear, I was going to stop by to see you next. I've just returned to town." He strode to her side to buss her cheek. "Don't you look lovely?"

She didn't feel lovely.

In truth, she no longer understood any of what was going on. "I did not realize you'd ever left London. My parents are in town. They were hoping to see you last night."

"I should have told you." He appeared sincerely contrite. "But Stoke and I had urgent business to attend to, and we had to leave quite suddenly. We thought to be back yesterday, but the matter took longer than expected to resolve." He muttered something about Lord Liverpool and a trade negotiation with the wool merchants' guild that sounded utterly fabricated to her ears.

But she had no business experience.

Every word of it might have been true.

"I only meant to drop Stoke back here, but then I was lured into viewing the new wallpaper your sister," he said, turning to bow over Dahlia's hand, "had ordered special and was being delivered today."

Seriously? He was lured by wallpaper?

She glanced at Dahlia. Not even her sister believed it.

He was still bowing over Dahlia's hand. "What a pleasant coincidence to see you here."

"Yes," Dahlia said wryly. "Saves you the bother of an extra trip to Chipping Way."

"It is never a bother." He turned to Heather. "Perhaps once we've returned from our wedding tour, your sister will help you redecorate our home. It ought to have your touch, don't you think?"

She blushed. "Yes, it is an excellent idea."

The entire conversation was utterly polite, and every word plausible, but not a bit of it rang true.

Heather said little, eager to be away from Tilbury, Stoke, and his daughter. She felt as though she were talking to strangers. "My sister and I must be off. We have another appointment."

It was a lie.

It tripped so easily off her tongue, and she said it while looking straight at Tilbury.

They were not yet married, and she was already lying to him. She suspected he was lying to her.

How could they start their married life this way? She had never considered being anything but honest with her husband. Of course, dashing off with Dahlia because they were going to eat pies was just a small fib.

But why would she feel the need to get away from the man she was going to pledge her life to in a matter of days? She wanted to insist they speak alone but did not want to say anything in front of Stoke or Lady Melinda.

She tried to implore him silently, but he did not seem to get the hint. They could not put off the discussion any longer.

They had to call off the wedding.

It had to be done by mutual agreement. She could not do it alone for fear he would sue her family for breach of promise. Her parents would lose everything they'd worked for over the years.

She left never feeling so ill in her life.

Within the hour, she and Dahlia were seated at Blakney's Confectionery eating their pies.

"Heather, you are going to choke if you don't stop cramming that apple crumble down your throat."

Her mouth was too full to immediately reply, but she nodded as she shoveled down more. Yes, that was it. She could eat herself sick and miss her wedding.

She glanced at Dahlia's plate and the cherry tart still on it, hardly picked. "I'll have your cherry tart if you don't want it, Dahlia."

Her sister grabbed her hand and held it still so that she could not stick her fork into the confection. "What is the matter with you? And don't you dare tell me it is nothing. We have to talk about this. You cannot turn into a runaway bride."

She nodded miserably. "All I want to do is talk to Tilbury before the wedding. I think he's purposely avoiding me. What was he doing at Stoke's home? And the other night at his ball, Stoke and his daughter were with him more than I was. Why are they suddenly the best of friends?"

"The best of friends…again. They've known each other since childhood." Dahlia dabbed her lips with her table linen. "It troubled me, too."

"And yet, Tilbury was ever the perfect gentleman. I don't know what to make of him. Not even Robbie doubts his integrity."

Dahlia nibbled her lip. "Ronan and Joshua like him, too. But there is no denying something is going on."

"Perhaps it is this mysterious business he and Stoke are handling on behalf of Lord Liverpool."

"Oh, Heather. I don't believe there is any business going on. At least, not anything parliamentary." Dahlia took a deep breath. "You're not going to like what I am thinking."

"Just say it. I need to figure out what is happening here."

"You're right." She took another deep breath. "I think it's about him and Lady Melinda. You know how there were rumors about her and a mysterious marquess?"

Heather nodded. "Poor Ronan was in the thick of it. He bore the brunt of her little schemes, constantly having his name linked to hers in the scandal sheets. She claimed it was all in fun, didn't she?"

"Yes," Dahlia said with a frown. "Supposedly to make a certain marquess jealous and lure him into proposing to her. I thought it was all made up. I was sure she was in love with someone else. And now I am worried that she was also manipulating me into believing...oh, good heavens. Do you think she's been after Tilbury all this time?"

Heather's heart shot into her throat. "Tell me everything you know. Every detail, no matter how inconsequential you believe it is."

"Of course." Dahlia shook her head. "I was certain she was in love with...oh, I dare not say."

Heather set aside her plate and cast her sister an imploring gaze. "Please. You *must* tell me everything."

Dahlia glanced around. "Not here. Let's stop at Holly's. We can talk there, undisturbed. And we may as well bring her in on the discussion. Mama and Papa aren't due back for hours yet."

But they had no sooner arrived and settled in the parlor than Joshua, Ronan, and Robbie marched in.

Robbie took one look at her and knew her dreams were falling apart. "Pixie, what's wrong? Has something happened to ye?"

CHAPTER TEN

ROBBIE TOOK A step forward, his instinct to take Heather in his arms. But she held out her hands to wave him off. "No, Robbie. Nothing is wrong."

"Well, there's a statement no one believes, lass." She looked so beaten down; he couldn't bear it.

She tipped her chin up in indignation. "It is no one's business. I can handle it myself."

"Yerself? And ye dinna wish for anyone else's help? Or is it just my help ye dinna want?" He hadn't meant to sound angry, but she was hurting, and he wanted to protect her. It did not sit well with him that she was doing her best to push him away. "Och, lass. What has Tilbury done?"

Her eyes rounded in surprise. "What makes you think—"

"Heather, stop." Dahlia was staring intently at her sister. "You're doing the same thing I did with Gerald Wainscott, thinking I was capable of handling the situation. Instead, I stood there like a spineless dimwit while he humiliated me in front of all my friends and family."

Dahlia glanced at her husband, and her expression immediately turned loving. "I should have let Ronan step up and hit him from the first. Not that I approve of violence, but Gerald would have been too busy dealing with his bloody nose to say all those hurtful things to me. I was so badly wounded by him, and Gerald and I were not even betrothed. Not only are you betrothed to Tilbury, but you are marrying him the day after tomorrow. This is not the time for your pride to get in the way."

Heather sank onto the settee and buried her face in her hands. "You're right. This is a nightmare."

"Blessed saints," Joshua muttered, running a hand through his hair. "Will someone tell me what is going on?"

"Shall I start?" Robbie said, staring at Heather and knowing what he was about to say would be hurtful to her. "We've tossed the question about, but nobody had the answer for it. I think I do now."

"What question, Robbie?" Heather asked, her words muffled because her face was still buried in her hands, and she would not lower them to look up at him.

"What is it Tilbury saw in ye to make him want to marry ye?" He tried to keep his voice gentle because he knew his next words were going to be unkind, and he desperately wished he did not have to wound her. "He saw Lady Melinda in ye, lass. This is why he offered for yer hand in marriage."

"Robbie? Is this true?" Holly was now gaping at him, her expression one of confusion.

"Aye, it's the truth. I've thought of nothing but Heather since the moment I set eyes on her. I've done nothing but look at her, think of her every chance I got. I've memorized the way she moves, the way she stands. For me to mistake Lady Melinda for her...well, that speaks to how closely Heather resembles her."

"But only from a distance," Ronan added. "Up close, talking to you, Heather, one would never mistake you for Melinda."

"Aye, lass. She does no' have yer entrancing eyes or yer beautiful smile." He expected Heather to be jumping up in outrage by now, but she did not jump. She did not flinch. She did not move a muscle. "Pixie, say something. I'm sorry if my words hurt ye. Of course, they hurt ye. I'd give anything for them not to be true. But I knew it the moment I walked into Tilbury's ballroom and mistook her for ye. She had her back to the door and was standing beside Tilbury. I was certain I was looking at ye."

He gave a laughing groan. "It was only when she turned around that I realized my error. It hit me like a bolt of lightning. This is why he chose ye. I could no' shake the feeling. I wished so desperately to be wrong. But I dinna think I am."

Dahlia sank onto the settee beside her sister and put her arms around her. However, she looked up at him as she spoke. "Oh, Robbie. This is why we came over to Holly's. We'd just come to the same realization. We did not want to believe it either. We hoped to get Holly's opinion, talk it out, and convince ourselves we were wrong."

Dahlia now turned to Ronan. "You once told me that Lady Melinda was manipulative, but I never realized to what lengths she would go. She had me convinced she was in love with someone else. I was sure of it. I felt so sorry for her."

Ronan nodded. "I know, love."

"It never occurred to me that she was... I still don't understand what she is doing—suddenly becoming my best friend. Working with me to redecorate her home. Was it all a ruse to keep me close and find out what was going on between Heather and Tilbury?"

Holly clasped her hands, now obviously fretting. "They are despicable. Both of them. Using my two younger sisters for their petty game." She drew a chair up beside Heather so that both her sisters were now flanking her and offering comfort. "Why would he simply not ask Lady Melinda to marry him?"

Ronan cleared his throat. "He very well may have offered for her, but she was still angry over losing her mother and perhaps angry with him for something he might have done, or said, or should have said. Who knows what might have passed between the two of them? But this is how she is. Tilbury might have innocently said or done something to offend her. However, since she was feeling pain, she had to make him hurt as well. By the time she came around to realizing what she had done, he'd found himself a Melinda look-alike in Heather. I know it is no consolation to you, Heather, but I think you are the far better choice. In time, he will come to realize it."

She lifted her head finally and gazed at Ronan in astonishment. "In time? No, I cannot marry him. But how do I get out of it now? I've been trying to get a hold of him for days in the hope we might talk, and do you know where he was? Chatting as calm as you please with the Duke of Stoke and Melinda. He spouted some nonsense about intending to call upon me next."

She gave a huff and continued, "He claimed to have just returned to London and stopped in at the Stoke residence to see the wallpaper Dahlia chose for their home. Wallpaper? While I sent him three notes over these past few days begging him to see me?"

She rolled her eyes. "He was caught unaware when we walked in. Our visit was unexpected and surprised him. He said the first thing that came into his mind and assured me ever so politely that he would call upon me. But I know he won't. He's been purposely avoiding me and will do so until he has to face me in church on our wedding day. But there won't be a wedding. I won't marry him."

Robbie let out the breath he hadn't realized he'd been holding. "Lass, do ye mean it? Ye will no' go through with the ceremony?"

She nodded. "How can I now?"

His heart soared, but only for the moment. It was one thing to wish to break off their betrothal, but there were dire consequences to such an action, especially if Tilbury meant to hold her to the promise to marry him.

If she refused, he could sue her parents and ruin them financially. He had the wealth and power to do it.

"I have to try to end it, Robbie. I don't know if I'll succeed. Perhaps if I reach out to Lady Melinda for help. She has a vested interest. She had to know the moment Tilbury proposed to me that he was sending her a message."

Dahlia looked quite troubled. "They've been using everyone, especially Heather and the Duke of Stoke's estate manager. That quiet, earnest fellow, James Dawson. He was the one she pretended to be in love with. Dear heaven, what this man must have been thinking!"

"Poor Mr. Dawson," Heather said, nodding. "He must have been quaking in his boots, worried that her little game would cause him to lose his position. All it would have taken was a careless word from Melinda, and the duke would have sacked him without references."

"Let's talk to Tilbury," Joshua said. "If it is a game to him, then it must now come to an end. I'll go to him. I'll bring Tynan with me. Ronan, you keep out of it. You already have a history with Melinda, and it will not help to have it dug up again. Robbie, you also have to keep out of it. You cannot be objective about the situation. You'll hit him, and that will only make matters worse. Perhaps I'll bring Tynan, Marcus, and James with me. The three Brayden earls."

"I dinna need ye fighting my battles." Robbie was not pleased to be shut out. "I've dealt with those Upper Crust arses all year long in Parliament. I know how to handle them."

Everyone rolled their eyes at him, even Heather. "It isn't your battle, Robbie. It's mine," she pointed out with irritating calm. "None of you will go with me. I won't have you risking your positions because you've angered Stoke and Tilbury. If Tilbury won't see me, then I'll turn to Dillie's husband, the Duke of Edgeware for help. I'll tell him what has happened and ask him to summon Tilbury...or come with me when I pay a call on Stoke. They can't touch him. He's too powerful."

"Will ye drag yer cousins and their husbands into this now?" Robbie frowned, not liking that the matter was being taken out of his control. He ought to be the one to get his hands on Tilbury. He supposed this is why none of them wanted him near the man.

They did not trust his temper.

But they were wrong. Heather mattered more to him than foolish pride. "We are all good at our positions as military liaisons because we know how to negotiate. Ye know I have good instincts and understand how to horse trade. All I have to do is offer Tilbury something he wants in exchange for something I want."

Indeed, it could be easily accomplished without having to punch, threaten, or abduct anyone. Tilbury wanted Melinda. He just needed to get the pair together and admitting they cared for each other. Then Tilbury would agree to release Heather from the unwanted betrothal.

He just wanted to keep the others out of the way and let him do whatever he needed to do to reach that goal.

Ronan frowned. "There's more involved with that pair than mere horse-trading."

Joshua agreed. "What if he isn't through playing his game?"

"Perhaps we should involve Edgeware," Holly said.

"Or Honey's husband, the Earl of Wycke," Dahlia interjected.

Robbie ran a hand through his hair in consternation as the others kept tossing out ideas that were considered and dismissed. "Enough," he finally said with a quiet authority that silenced everyone. "Ye need to let me handle the matter. Heather's not to go to Edgeware or Wycke, even if they are family and will agree to help. No one's to go to them. In fact, ye're to leave them completely out of it. I dinna need their assistance. Heather, even ye have to stay out of the way for now."

She was not pleased with the suggestion. "It is my life at stake. Shouldn't I have a say in the negotiations?"

"Ye've had it. Ye dinna want the marriage. Thank the Graces ye came around to it in time. I think I would have made an arse of myself if ye hadn't."

She tipped her head and eyed him quizzically. "What would you have done?"

"Not sure. For all the talk about wanting only yer happiness, the truth of the matter is that I'm a possessive arse, and I wanted ye to be happy with me and no one else. I dinna think I could have given ye up to another, especially if I thought ye dinna love the man ye were about to marry or he dinna love ye."

"Which he doesn't. We all understand this now. You would have stopped the ceremony?"

He nodded. "Aye, lass."

"How?"

He shrugged. "Possibly stormed the church on Gallant, swept ye up into the saddle, and headed off to Scotland with ye."

Her eyes widened. "Robbie, that's absurd."

"Well, ye asked me. Aye, it is absurd. Barbaric. Scandalous. Bound to have serious repercussions. My imprisonment, for certain."

Heather shot to her feet. "I'd never allow that to happen. No, Robbie. No matter what happens between now and the wedding, you cannot steal me away or do anything that will lead to your imprisonment. All the more reason why Edgeware and I must be the ones to—"

"No! Ye're a stubborn lass. Tilbury's already using ye as a hostage, and ye dinna even realize it. He's been dangling ye in front of Lady Melinda and her father all this time. Why do ye think Stoke was suddenly our best friend on the night of Tilbury's ball? It is because he knows his daughter and Tilbury love each other, and now he is running out of time to match them properly."

Holly frowned. "Tilbury's the one who put them in this mess by offering to marry Heather. Why hasn't he broken it off with my sister yet?"

"Because he still needs his hostage. Likely Lady Melinda has no' accepted him yet."

Joshua regarded him with some surprise. "The bloody blackguard! Is it possible he's proposed to Melinda while still betrothed and about to marry Heather?"

Robbie ran a hand through his hair. "Aye. Possible. Probable. And he's purposely keeping the pressure on Melinda by not breaking off his betrothal to Heather. This is his leverage in the negotiation."

"Stoke must be livid," Joshua said. "Do you think you can get him on your side?"

Robbie nodded. "I hope so. Our interests are united in this. Neither of us wants to see the wedding take place." He turned to Heather. "Lass, ye must keep away from yer betrothed. Stay out of his sight, and let me handle him."

Joshua and Ronan finally relented and backed him up.

Heather felt bloodied and wounded. "How can you agree with Robbie?"

"Because he's right," Ronan said gently.

She had already crossed the parlor to fetch her bonnet and gloves but set them back down and reluctantly nodded. "Robbie, will you promise me not to punch him?"

Robbie smiled at her. "I can promise ye I'll not be the one to throw the first punch. But if he strikes me, I'll be defending myself. He won't hit me, though. This is not Tilbury's way. As I said, he's a negotiator. But so am I, and I'm better at it than he is. He's boxed himself into a corner with all his wily schemes. I'm going to help him out of that corner, give him an opening he can take."

Heather cast him a stubborn look. "My wedding is the day after tomorrow."

"Och, lass. I'm aware of every minute that passes." He studied her face, aching because she was beautiful even when she was obstinate. But when her expression softened, and he saw her vulnerability, he did not think there was a more beautiful woman alive.

"I'm so sorry for creating this mess, Robbie."

"Dinna shoulder the blame, lass. Had I opened my eyes, had I listened to my heart, I could have fought for ye, courted ye, and avoided all this. But I dinna, so here we are now, trying our best to climb out of the hole we've dug for ourselves."

His words did little to soothe her. He felt the misery still pouring out of her.

"You are being kind to me. I am solely to blame. I'm the one who shut my eyes and closed off my heart. You tried to warn me. I wouldn't listen."

"Pixie, no. I allowed ye to ignore me. I rode away for months because it was easier to give ye over to someone else than deal with the problems we'd have to face if we were to marry. I'm still worried about them. I fully appreciate all ye'd be giving up if we were to wed. Love alone is no' enough to sustain us. Ye'd need to trust me as well, and that would be a leap of faith on yer part. How can ye believe in me when I've spent my life behaving like an arse and earning my wicked reputation?"

"None of it will matter if I am doomed to marry Tilbury. Let's deal with him first. What is the adage? Be careful what you wish for? Well, I got my wished-for marquess, and now I must face the possibility that the wish I've carried in my heart since I was five years old may come true."

"Not if I can help it," Robbie said with a steely resolve, for Tilbury would have to kill him before that ever happened. Such talk would only overset Heather, so he said nothing. Anyway, he doubted matters would get physical. Tilbury was not the sort to get his hands dirty. It was not the man's style.

In truth, Tilbury probably thought they could talk it over like gentlemen.

"Robbie, please be careful. I couldn't bear it if my mistakes destroyed your life, too."

Robbie cupped her chin and gently tilted her face upward so she could look him in the eye. "Do ye love me, Heather?"

She winced and squirmed and finally nodded. "Yes. I do."

"Then it is settled, lass. There will be no marriage to the marquess. Tilbury is no' getting his hands on ye. If he refuses to budge, then dinna be surprised by what happens next."

Her pixie eyes rounded in alarm. "Robbie, please. I couldn't live with myself if you were hurt."

"And I could not live with myself if ye were forced into a marriage ye dinna want. Too late to change my mind, lass. I'll do whatever I must." He frowned at his friends. "Dinna think to stop me. Gallant's a warhorse. He'll trample ye under his hooves. If ye want to help, then keep out of my way."

Heather gasped. "I forbid you—"

"Save yer breath for my kisses, Heather. Ye love me, and that's all I need to hear. He is no' getting his hands on ye. I'm marrying ye first. I dinna care if they hang me later for stealing ye away."

"But I care! Don't be a stubborn Scot."

He dipped his head and kissed her with every bit of stubborn Scottish pride in him. He also kissed her with every bit of love he felt for her.

He tasted the sweetness of her lips, felt them give against the pressure of his own, and deepened the kiss. But he drew away soon after, for the sweetest, most potent kisses would have to wait until they were alone.

"Robbie," she whispered once he had released her, "promise me you won't put yourself in danger for me."

"I canno' do that, lass. Do ye no' realize what ye mean to me?"

"It doesn't matter."

"Aye, it does. Pixie, you are my very heart. It does no' beat without ye."

CHAPTER ELEVEN

"CAPTAIN ROBERT MACLAUREN," said Tilbury's formidable butler, announcing Robbie as he was led into the marquess's study.

Tilbury rose and greeted him with a wry smile. "Welcome, Captain MacLauren. I was wondering when you were going to come around to see me."

"I'm here now, and since we both know what this is about," Robbie said, taking the offered seat in front of Tilbury's desk and waiting for him to take the one behind the desk before proceeding, "what is it ye want in exchange for Heather's release from the betrothal?"

"It does not bear discussion. It isn't going to happen."

Robbie arched an eyebrow, trying his best not to respond to Tilbury's intractability by pounding his fist into the man's face. "My lord, we both know yer heart belongs to Lady Melinda. So why the need to drag Heather into whatever game the two of ye are playing?"

The marquess leaned back in his chair and briefly closed his eyes before opening them again. "Unfortunately, this is quite a serious matter. If I knew a way to have a happy outcome for us all, I would leap at it. But there isn't. Lady Melinda will not have me."

"So ye will grab second best? Heather is no man's second best. Ye'll break her heart if ye marry her."

Tilbury cast him an impatient glance. "She'll be a marchioness. I'll be generous with her, and she will not want for anything. Once I have my heirs, she can do as she wishes."

"Then ye only intend to use her as a breeder?"

"MacLauren, don't be crass. I'll impose myself on her as little as possible. Of course, it will be necessary for the first few years. But afterward, no. She'll have my name. We'll be seen at all the important functions together. She won't lack companionship since she has her sisters and a horde of cousins in town to keep her entertained. I know how to be discreet. All I'll ask of her is to be discreet in her affairs as well."

Robbie clenched his jaw and silently counted to ten. "She is no' the sort to ever stray from her wedding vows. She'll be faithful to ye to her dying day, even if it means her living with a broken heart to the end of her days."

"Aren't you being a bit theatrical? She'll adapt to—"

"The lass wants a husband who will be faithful to her and with whom she can make a life. She is no' interested in a marriage in name only. She does no' want yer wealth or title. She wants love." He leaned forward. "So, I'll repeat my question. What is it ye want in exchange for releasing Heather from the betrothal?"

Tilbury shook his head despairingly. "I want Lady Melinda. But I've just told you, she will not have me."

"Did she give ye a reason why she will no' have ye? Because if ye ask me, she would no' have been engaging in her own games concerning her mysterious marquess if she dinna care for ye."

He sighed. "Very well. What harm can there be in confessing all to you know? She will not have me because of the stupidest reason I've ever heard. I did not know her favorite flower, nor did I know her favorite color. What the hell is that about? Who refuses a proposal over something so trivial?"

"My lord, with all due respect...ye're a bloody *idjit*."

"What!"

"Calm down and hear me out." Robbie was astounded by the

man's utter lack of awareness. "It is no' about colors or flowers. It's that ye dinna bother to consider her likes or bother to learn what matters to her. I'm a big arse, and yet I know this. If I may be blunt, my lord?"

"Blunter than you already have been? I could have you tossed out for calling me an idiot."

"But ye know ye have been behaving like one. If ye thought otherwise, I wouldn't still be seated here."

Tilbury sighed and gave a curt nod. "Go ahead. We're running out of time. I don't want niceties. I want solutions."

"Lady Melinda needs to know ye love her. Have ye told her? Have ye kissed her? Have ye let her know she's the most important thing to ye?"

"Of course, I have." But he began to fidget. "Perhaps not in so many words, but I offered to marry her. Doesn't this say it all?"

"Ye offered to marry Heather, too. And ye dinna love her. So why should Lady Melinda think ye're behaving like a man in love and not merely a petulant, manipulative, sore loser?"

"Now, see here, MacLauren! Do you want to work this out or just insult me?" He ran a hand through his hair. "What do I need to do?"

Gad! Never in his wildest dreams did Robbie believe he'd be teaching the marquess all he'd learned from *The Book of Love*. Nor did he ever think the marquess could be so inept when it came to matters of the heart. But his parents were likely not a love match, for few among the Upper Crust considered it as important as consolidating wealth.

He almost felt sorry for Tilbury. Although he had all the trappings and advantages of his rank, he'd probably never had a mother's uncompromising love or a father's guidance on matters other than the duties of a marquess and how to keep the Tilbury coffers stuffed. "Ye're going to start by making lists."

"Lists? What sort of lists? And whatever for?"

"The first list is going to be about the five senses. Sight, touch, taste, hearing, scent. Ye'll take each sense and write down all the things ye like about Lady Melinda. For example, for sight...what did ye notice first about the look of her, what do ye like best about her? Rest assured, this list is between us only. Ye can be crass. If ye like her breasts, write it down."

"In detail?"

Was he serious? "Aye," Robbie said, deciding it was best not to censor him. "Size. Shape. Perkiness. Fullness. All of it."

He watched as Tilbury withdrew parchment and quill pen from his desk drawer. In truth, he was surprised by the man's eagerness to follow his instructions. Perhaps it boded well for a good outcome, but Robbie was no' going to hold his breath. "If ye like her face, list what ye like about it. The curve of her lips. The twinkle in her eyes."

Tilbury laughed. "Melinda's eyes do not twinkle."

"Did they used to?"

"Yes, when we were younger. But not for several years now." He put his hands to his face and groaned. "Are you saying I'm the cause for her unhappiness?"

"Likely one of the more important causes. Now we know this is one of the things ye need to do. Put the sparkle back in her eyes. By the way, what color are they?"

"Her eyes? A bluish-gray. What of it?"

Robbie shrugged. "Just making sure ye know at least that about her."

"I'm not completely blind, you know. She happens to have beautiful eyes. So how do I put the sparkle back in them?"

"Easy." Did this man know nothing about women? "Make yerself enough of an arse over her that she canno' help the smile reaching into her eyes. But let's get back to the lists. Before ye start writing down yer thoughts, I need ye to send a footman to fetch Dahlia Brayden and bring her here."

He frowned. "Why? You aren't going to show her what I'm scribbling here, are you?"

"No, my lord. I promised ye those lists are between us alone. Once we've discussed them, ye can burn them. We need Dahlia because, unlike ye, she knows Lady Melinda's favorite color and her favorite flower. She's been listening to the lass, whereas, ye've been deaf as a post."

"Stop insulting me."

"Has politeness helped ye get what ye want?"

Tilbury grumbled. "No. But it still doesn't mean you can insult me." He remained grumbling as he rang for his butler and instructed him to send a footman and his carriage to pick up Dahlia.

Robbie knew he was being impatient with Tilbury, who was not a terrible man. But he was doing a terrible thing and needed to be stopped. They had only one day left to rectify what had taken years to mess up. Perhaps it was too late to fix all that had passed between him and Lady Melinda. But one thing for certain, he was not going to stop trying until Heather was released from their betrothal. "My lord, I beg yer forgiveness in advance. I'm not purposely trying to insult ye. I like ye and have a deep respect for ye. Ye've always been fair in yer dealings with me, and for this I am grateful."

He grunted. "I happen to respect you, too. I would not have allowed you into my home otherwise. You're an honest man, MacLauren. There aren't too many of them around."

"I know. But let's get back to this assignment. Ye have to let go of yer civilized feelings. We have only a day to convince Lady Melinda that ye love her. Politeness is no' going to do it. Making a complete and utter donkey's arse of yerself over her is yer only recourse now. And I speak from experience. When it comes to Heather, I seem to do this quite easily and quite often. But I would die for the lass, and she knows it."

Tilbury nodded. "And Melinda needs to know this is what I would do for her?"

"Aye. Nothing less." He stared at the parchment. "Start yer lists because there's more I need to teach ye."

"Such as what?"

"I'll tell ye after ye've made yer lists."

"Very well." Tilbury laughed mirthlessly and gazed at the bottles of brandy, bourbon, and wine on display in an ornate cabinet tucked in the corner of his study. Also on display were crystal decanters and glasses obviously of the finest quality. "Help yourself to my stock while we work, MacLauren. I expect this is thirsty business. Would you mind pouring me a port wine? I think I'm going to need the fortification as I work."

"Verra well. To quench yer thirst. But ye canno' get falling-down drunk."

Tilbury arched an eyebrow. "What are you, my nursemaid?"

"Aye, if I have to be. But mostly, I'm the man who loves Heather enough to get on my knees and kiss yer hairy arse if it will get ye to end yer betrothal to her. And this is what Lady Melinda needs to feel ye'd do for her. Anything less, and we'll have a problem."

"Forget the wine. Pour me a brandy. Make it a double."

"Start writing. I want to be done talking over these lists with ye before Dahlia arrives."

To Robbie's relief, Tilbury eagerly dove into his assignment and finished rather quickly. Tilbury was clever in most things, but not in his dealings with women. Still, he hoped the speed with which he completed the assignment did not signify a lack of thought.

Or worse, did it signify a lack in his ability to feel passion?

This would be a problem.

How was the man going to inspire rapture and desire in Melinda if he was a cold fish?

He took a moment to peruse what Tilbury had written down, curious about what his lists would reveal. He tried not to laugh out loud as he reviewed them.

Blessed saints.

The marquess was a molten, roiling, volcanic mess over Melinda. How did he manage to keep his feelings so well hidden? He'd even revealed that he had plucked her cherry when the lass was seventeen. Not only plucked it but savored the juices, rolled it in his tongue. Inhaled her. Memorized the taste and touch of her.

Gad! Too much information.

Even he was blushing, and he'd seen and done just about every-thing there was to do, sometimes with more than one lusty, willing lass at a time.

But he could not criticize the marquess for pouring his thoughts onto paper. The man was desperate for help. Also apparent was that he never intended the betrothal to Heather to get this far.

And yet, he was determined to have her if he could not have Melinda.

This was their biggest problem.

What if Lady Melinda refused him today and then turn around in a week and decide she loved him after all? That was the disaster they all needed to avoid and could if Tilbury was not stubbornly refusing to let go of Heather until he had Melinda in hand.

Robbie had not ruled out conspiring with Tilbury to abduct Melinda and escort the pair to Gretna Green if it came down to it. But this was something he was loath to suggest since it would mean remaining in their company for days, and he'd probably be hanged for the favor afterward anyway.

Besides, Heather would not be too pleased about his behavior even if he did avoid hanging, which he doubted was likely since Stoke was a duke and would be out for someone's blood. Since it would not be Tilbury's, it would be his Scottish blood they'd slowly drain from his body.

"Well? What do you think, MacLauren?"

"A commendable job, my lord. I can see ye love the lass and know her well. I also know from the conversation ye were having with her and the duke at yer ball that ye have a long history with them. That is good. It is these connections that bind a husband and wife together. Where ye fail is in the expectations."

Tilbury placed his elbows on his desk and leaned forward, eager to hear whatever it was Robbie had to tell him. The man was earnest, he had to give him that. "What do you mean by expectations?"

"Ye've disappointed her ever since ye…claimed her. She dinna merely give her body to ye back then. She gave ye her heart. And what did ye do with that gift?"

Tilbury cleared his throat. "I offered to marry her."

"When? Three years later? Did ye approach her or her father first? And what did ye do in the years in between?"

He sat upright and cast him an indignant glance. "I had duties that I could not shirk. I was a new marquess. It was not easy for me, either."

Robby had also poured himself a brandy and was about to take a sip but set it down instead. "What duties, my lord? Counting yer cattle? Collecting yer revenue from the towns under yer charter? Attending yer fancy balls and soirees? What was so important that ye left the lass to her broken heart?"

"I made it right as soon as I could," he said, his defense sounding quite feeble.

"Ye dinna make it right. She still has no' accepted ye. So are ye going to sit here and make excuses, or are ye going to own up to yer mistakes and seize yer happiness?"

"And what of Heather? She's a sweet girl. She'll be humiliated and made a laughingstock if your plan works. Why would you do this to her?"

"I'll take care of Heather. Any scandal will quickly die out once all of us are happily matched. Ye know it will take very little for the *ton* to lose interest when all parties are happy. It is humiliation and misery that appeals to them. At the end of the day, ye've jilted a commoner, and everyone will be relieved ye and Lady Melinda have finally come to yer senses. As for Heather, she already knows I will do whatever it takes to protect her. I'll not let her be hurt."

He nodded. "And this is how I need to make Melinda feel."

"Right."

They said nothing more as Dahlia hurried in, escorted by Ronan. "What do you want with my wife?"

Robbie and Tilbury both rose and offered Dahlia the seat beside Robbie's. "Ye canno' be in here, Ronan. Wait in the visitors' parlor. We will no' keep her long."

He folded his arms across his chest. "What do you need her for?"

"I need her help," Tilbury said with his typically calm demeanor. "Ballard will see you are made comfortable while you wait. Nothing sinister will go on, I promise. We need a woman's opinion and advice, that's all. Captain MacLauren suggested your wife, and I agree it is an excellent idea. She is clever. Knowledgeable. Or do you not believe she is capable of—"

"Of course, she's capable." He glanced at Dahlia, his expression quite defeated. "Call out to me if you want to leave."

She smiled up at him, her eyes shining with love for Ronan. "I'll be fine."

He followed Ballard out, but not before casting Robbie and Tilbury a warning glance.

"Did ye see the look on his face?" Robbie asked Tilbury.

"Do you mean the one where he silently threatened to tear us to pieces if we took a toe out of step with his wife? That look?" He chuckled. "Yes."

"Good. That's the look of a man who loves his wife."

Dahlia took her seat and regarded each of them quizzically. "He was behaving like an arrogant dolt." She shook her head and grinned. "You won't tell him I just said that, will you, Robbie?"

"No. Are ye really angry with him?"

"Of course not. I love him. But I expect that's obvious. He needn't be so protective of me, that's all. He knows I am in safe hands with you." She folded her hands on her lap. "How can I help?"

"Ye need to tell us all ye know about Lady Melinda. What she likes. What she dislikes. Let's start with the obvious first. Her favorite color. Her favorite flower. What foods she likes. Things of that nature."

She eyed the marquess thoughtfully. "Is this what all the fuss is about? You didn't know her favorite color? Or her favorite flower?"

Tilbury nodded. "How am I to know this? I don't go about asking my friends those questions. They're dull and idiotic...the questions, I mean. Not my friends. They are not dull or idiotic, or they would not be my friends."

"You did not need to ask her," Dahlia replied gently. "Did you not see the wallpaper we ordered? You made a point of mentioning it to Heather and me when we last saw you at the Duke of Stoke's residence. But you were lying through your teeth about your reason for stopping there, and we all knew it. You are quite amazing, my lord."

Tilbury arched an eyebrow. "Why do I not feel a compliment coming on?"

"Because I'm about to berate you. Your glib lie broke Heather's heart as well as Lady Melinda's heart. Shall I explain how?"

"Yes," he said, rubbing his temples. "I am very bad at this sort of thing."

"What? At telling the truth? This is all either of them ever wanted from you. Yet you lied to Heather about your reason for stopping at His Grace's residence when you knew she was desperate to speak to you. And then you broke Lady Melinda's heart by using the wallpaper as an excuse, not even realizing she chose it because it was her favorite flower and her favorite color. Do you even know what it was? Can

THE HEART OF LOVE

you even guess now? Obviously not, or I would not have been summoned. You managed to hurt two women with one lie. Quite impressive."

"Mrs. Brayden, I have not been spanked so thoroughly since I was a child of four."

She tipped her head up in defiance. "Are you expecting an apology from me? You will not have one. You are about to break my sister's heart for insisting on holding to this farce of a betrothal, and for no reason other than you want to hurt the woman you really love. So forgive me if I am insolent. But I believe I am showing remarkable restraint. What I'd really like to do is punch you in the nose."

Robbie groaned. "Dahlia, will ye kindly tell us her favorite color and flower? I dinna need a brawl to break out here."

She sniffed. "Very well. Her favorite color is lavender, and her favorite flower is the lilac because it represents first love. *First love.* Is this significant to you in any way? She was trying to send a message to you, her first love who is dense as a post and has no care for her feelings."

"Och, Dahlia. Will ye stop spanking the man? But this gives me an idea. My lord, do ye want to make a grand gesture she'll understand and appreciate?"

"Yes. What must I do?"

Robbie turned to Dahlia. "All flowers have a meaning, do they not?"

Dahlia nodded. "Oh, I see what you're getting at. My lord, I think you must take a trip to Camden Town and buy up all the red flowers available. But I think you are too late to do it today. The flower vendors set up quite early. You must visit first thing tomorrow morning. Salvia, tulips, carnations. All red because this is the color of love. Salvia tells her that you are thinking of her. Red salvia tells her that you are hers forever. Carnations are the long-revered flower of love in ancient civilizations. She will know this, so you must include carnations. Tulips are for romantic love. But you must also have lilacs—lots of them. Every lilac to be found in London. This is because she must be your first and only love, and this is how you tell her so that she believes you mean it."

"Will you accompany me, Mrs. Brayden? I know I cannot accomplish this on my own. It is not the best area, although I believe it will be safe enough once the sun rises. I'll bring along several footmen, and your husband may join us if he is concerned for your safety."

She nodded. "Thank you, but I'll explain it to him. He won't be available to come with us since he must report to the Admiralty first thing in the morning."

"Then you will join us?"

"I would do anything for the sake of my sister's happiness...something she will not have if she is forced to marry you."

"Och, Dahlia," Robbie said, emitting another groan. "Stop thrashing the man. What about a bride token? If he's going to wage a full-on assault, he'll need this, too."

"A blue sapphire ring or necklace. The blue sapphire represents loyalty, honesty, and faithfulness. This is your way of telling her that she can trust you."

Tilbury still appeared dejected. "How can it possibly work? She knows I don't know the first thing about colors or flowers or gems and what they signify other than to give as trinkets to some female I'm chasing after. She will immediately suspect I've been helped out, and these ideas came from someone other than me."

Robbie frowned. "They are no' trinkets. They are symbols of yer love. If ye treat them as baubles, then it will all be for naught. The point of the gesture is to show her ye are mad for her. She will no' care who gave ye the idea, only that ye thought enough of her to turn to others for help and were willing to do it because these things matter to *her*. She'll appreciate that ye bought out the Camden flower vendors for *her*. And another thing…"

"What more is there?" he muttered, once more rubbing his temples.

"Ye'd better have a few diamonds around that sapphire ring."

He glanced up, looking quite perplexed. "Why?"

"Because when she remarks on it, ye're going to tell her that the sapphire is yer sacred oath that ye will love her and be faithful to her forever. But the diamonds are there because they remind ye of the sparkle in her eyes the first time ye kissed her. Do ye think ye can do this?"

"Yes, Captain MacLauren. Contrary to what you and Mrs. Brayden think, I am not a complete and utter idiot."

Dahlia made a sound remarkably like a snort. "Oh, I—"

"Och, Dahlia. The comment does not call for a response. His lordship and I will pick ye up at nine o'clock tomorrow morning. Is that all right?"

She nodded. "Yes. I'll be ready. Is there anything else you need from me before I return to my fretting husband?"

Robbie laughed. "Just tell us anything else ye think might help us."

"Us? Why are the two of you suddenly thick as thieves? I was afraid you would be killing each other."

Tilbury cast a glance in Robbie's direction. "No, Mrs. Brayden. Although it might come down to that if Lady Melinda is still refusing my suit."

"Do you mean to say you would still go through with marrying my sister?" She gripped the arms of her chair.

Robbie was worried Dahlia might actually pick it up and toss it at the marquess. He was itching to do the same, but not yet. While there was a plan, there was hope. "Och, Dahlia. Think of this as a present-day *A Midsummer Night's Dream*. The parties who ought to be together are not. But it will all be sorted out in time. Everyone will wake on the day of the wedding and be united with their right true love."

She did not appear convinced. "Let's hope so. I shall be carrying weapons and will not hesitate to use them. I think I've given you enough information to work with for now. Call upon me if you find you need anything more. Otherwise, I shall see you gentlemen tomorrow morning."

Robbie waited for Ballard to escort her back to Ronan and show them both out before he turned to the marquess. "That went well," he said, his voice dripping with sarcasm.

"Do you think she'll follow through on her threat?"

Robbie shrugged. "To hurt ye if ye dinna release Heather from her promise to marry ye? Aye. And I may have to hold ye down while she does it. But we'll cross that path when we come to it." He raised his glass of brandy. "Here's hoping we never do."

"Don't you start on me, MacLauren. I'm not going to crumple under your threats either. So let's just try to convince Melinda I'm not as big an arse as she thinks I am."

"Right, let's get on with the next lesson," Robbie said, barely holding his temper in check. The marquess was wrong to think he'd ever get his hands on Heather. Robbie would make it clear to the man with his fists if it came to that. "Yer next lists will be about connections and expectations. What do ye have in common that will bind ye to each other? That ought to be easy. Ye grew up together and probably shared many things for the first time, and I dinna mean merely the physical encounters. A walk down a country lane on a beautiful day. A ride across a flower-dotted meadow. Sailing a skiff along a lake."

Tilbury cast him a wry grin. "Captain MacLauren, I never knew you were a romantic. Will you have me spouting poetry next?"

"If this is what Lady Melinda enjoys, then yes. Ye'll do it because she likes it, and ye care enough about her to want to please her. Is there something about this ye do not understand?"

He grunted. "I'm trying my best. You weren't raised being told you are the sun god and everyone ought to be kissing your arse. But I was. Only they neglected to mention that this rule does not apply to my wife and that I have to expend some effort to please her."

"Well, ye've learned the lesson now. She's to be yer partner, not yer servant. Once ye've written down all the ways ye are connected, then ye'll start on yer next list. Expectations. Which ye now understand must be adjusted if ye're to give her the happy marriage she's obviously been longing for. Give it some thought. And most important, consider her expectations as well as yer own. Are they the same as hers or divergent? If divergent, then what are ye willing to concede to make her happy?"

Tilbury took a large swallow of his brandy, then set the glass down on his desk and stared at it. "Sweet mother of mercy. How much more is there?"

"Quite a bit more. We're going to keep working on ye until the desire to please her comes naturally to ye. This must be yer heart's deepest wish. Ye must feel it in yer bones, that instinct to put her needs above yer own. A moment's hesitation, a moment of petulance, and ye'll lose her."

Tilbury sank back in his chair and groaned. "I think I'm going to need a refill."

CHAPTER TWELVE

ROBBIE KNEW IT was inappropriately late to stop by Romulus and Violet's residence. But Heather was staying there until her wedding day, and he needed to see her after spending the day with Tilbury. He knew she wouldn't mind. Indeed, she'd be desperate to learn what progress had been made.

Kicking Tilbury's pampered arse into shape had given him a monumental headache. However, an odd thing had happened as he'd tried to train the man to be a proper husband. He found that he was also teaching himself.

If only he and Heather had read the blasted book together instead of finding every which way to ignore it, all of this might have been avoided.

But they hadn't, now leaving him to deal with Tilbury's rock-hard, stubborn determination to marry Heather if he could not have Lady Melinda. He hoped it was merely Tilbury's way of keeping leverage on all of them. Obviously, the man was a fish out of water when it came to matters of romance. He was afraid to be left alone to drown in his ineptitude the moment he released Heather from their betrothal.

Robbie grunted as he knocked on the front door, suddenly struck by a thought. If Tilbury was only remaining stubborn in order to maintain leverage, could he sway the man by giving him a sacred oath to help him court Stoke's daughter in exchange for Heather's release?

He did not know if Tilbury would accept the proposal. Likely not.

Tilbury was after a victorious outcome, not merely the hope of one. Still, he'd raise the matter tomorrow. They'd be no worse off if he refused. Also, there was no harm in putting the idea into his head on the chance he might weaken and give in.

Romulus's butler opened the door to him. "Captain MacLauren, I'm afraid Captain Brayden and Mrs. Brayden have retired for the evening."

"And Miss Farthingale?"

The butler's expression softened. "She's in the library."

His tension eased, knowing she must have purposely been waiting up for him on the chance he would stop by to see her before heading back to his grandfather's townhouse. "Let her know I'm here."

He hadn't long to wait before Heather hurried forward to greet him, her pixie eyes wide and shimmering. "I was about to give up hope you would come by. Are you hungry? Thirsty?"

"No, lass. I'm fine. I wanted to see yer beautiful face before I went home. How are ye faring? I won't stay long."

She placed her arm in his and escorted him back into the library, allowing him to close the door behind them. Romulus's butler was not going to say anything, except perhaps to Romulus.

She turned to Robbie, her hopeful expression fading. "Oh, dear. I can see by the look on your face that he is still refusing to let me go. What's next? I want to bang his head against his finely built, elegant walls. Why is he being such a stubborn dolt?"

He tried to sound confident and not look downhearted. "We still have time, lass. He's doing his best to make things right."

She looked surprised. "You're on his side now?"

"Never. Always on yers."

She leaned her head against his shoulder, a sign of her dismay. But she only rested it there a moment before drawing away to look up at him, her eyes swallowing him up. "I know you're doing your best. Sit down and tell me how the day went. Are you sure I cannot get you something to eat?"

"Pixie, no. All I need is to look at ye." He held her back as she was about to take a seat.

She cast him an affectionate smile. "Why are you looking at me that way, Robbie?"

He must have had the stupidest grin on his face, but he was tired and strained, and yet looking at Heather elated him as nothing else could.

All felt right and good when he was with her.

"Och, lass. I'm just happy to be with ye." He took her in his arms, wanting to hold her sweet, soft body close to his. "What were ye reading?"

She made no protest, happily burrowing against his chest. "You'll think it's silly. *A Midsummer Night's Dream*, Shakespeare's play about mismatched lovers. But it ends happily, all the couples properly matched by the end of the story. It's us, isn't it? And I keep hoping that we'll all wake up to the same happy ending."

He laughed softly. "I was thinking the very same thing. I mentioned the play to Tilbury. We all want this to end right. He's just being an arse about it. But there's hope. I'll tell ye about our meeting after I kiss ye. Do ye mind, lass? I really need to kiss ye."

"I don't mind. I was hoping you would." Her smile lit up his heart. "Please do, Robbie."

She closed her eyes and tipped her head up. Her hands were at his chest, clutching the jacket of his uniform.

He lowered his head and pressed his lips to hers, wanting to be gentle. But her smile was magic, and she had the face of an angel. She overwhelmed him. He would never give her up, and he ached at the mere thought that he might have no choice.

He wanted her so badly.

All of her, all the time.

Not a few, stolen moments.

The gentle pressure turned into a desperate, crushing need. He wanted to swallow her into him, absorb all of her. Never let her go.

He tried to ease up when he thought he might be exerting too much pressure and hurting her, but she held him firm. Her warm lips sought his with aching urgency, and her beautiful body melted into his as though knowing she belonged to him, and no other man would ever claim her.

Aye, she belonged to him just as he belonged to her.

He'd been drumming the five senses into Tilbury's head all day, and now they flooded his own thoughts. He circled his arms around Heather's small waist to hold her close, needing to soak in her delicious scent and vibrant warmth. He tasted honey on her lips from the tea she'd been drinking.

He breathed in the subtle fragrance of lavender on her skin.

She was soft to the touch.

He undid the pins from her hair, not caring that they'd later be searching for them, wherever they silently dropped on the carpet.

He ran his fingers through the majestic waves of her golden-brown mane, loving the silken feel of it. *"Heether,* I love ye."

He felt her sob against his mouth as he kissed her again and again, unable to get enough of her and desperately wanting all of her. He nibbled her earlobe. He kissed her closed eyes, her throat, and the little pulse at the base of it.

He suckled the little pulse, skimming and swirling his tongue along it, sucking lightly on it to taste her skin, which was as sweet as morning dew.

His fingers found the buttons of her gown and undid them. Would she stop him?

He groaned as she, in turn, began to struggle with the buttons of his jacket. *"Mo chridhe.* We had better stop."

She inhaled lightly. "Did you just call me your love?"

It had slipped out, but he felt no shame in it, for this is what she was. "Aye, lass. I did." He knew he should go no further. This isn't what he'd intended. Not to take her up against bookshelves or upon a too-small settee.

He wanted the right to claim her as a husband had the right to claim his wife. Properly, lawfully, no shame involved on her part. And yet, he wanted her with a hunger that ravaged his soul.

He slid her gown down over one creamy shoulder and kissed her there. Aye, she was as sweet as a morning flower. He slid the gown a little lower and kissed the swell of her soft, pink breast. "Och, Pixie. Stop me. I dinna have the strength to do it myself."

She made no move.

Quite the opposite, she now had her hands plunged in his hair and was tugging on a fistful to hold him in place while he freed her breasts from the barrier of her clothing. As soon as they were bared to his view, he put his lips to suckle one ripe mound and then the other.

Blessed saints!

He felt her shudder as he swirled his tongue over the taut buds, licking and teasing them and delighting in her breathless moans. She clutched his head in innocent passion, not understanding her body's response...but being incredibly responsive to his touch.

She held him to her bosom, insistent as he continued to set flame to her body.

"Robbie, I want to feel your skin against mine," she said, moaning. "I want to run my hands along your body and feel your heat."

"Och, Pixie–"

She threw her arms around his neck and quietly began to sob. "If we are not meant to be together, if I'm to have nothing of you, then I need to remember you. I need to touch you and hold you and breathe you into my soul."

He felt the same, for he had a massive hole in his heart that only her love could fill. "Dinna cry. Ye'll tear my heart to pieces."

"Robbie, it's all my fault. I've made such a mess of everything."

"Lass, it took all four of us to create this problem. You, me. Tilbury and Melinda. Stop putting the blame on yer shoulders."

"I can't help it. All I had to do was refuse his proposal."

"And he dinna have to ask ye in the first place. Nor did Melinda have to reject him before he offered for ye to spite her. Nor did I have to leave London for months when all I ever wanted was to be with ye."

He eased her out of his arms and gently ran his thumbs across her cheeks to wipe away her tears. She was still exposed to him, her gown slipped to her waist and her chemise undone to bare her creamy mounds. Suddenly shy, she meant to draw the fabric over herself, but he stopped her. "No, lass. Not yet."

He took off his jacket and shirt, his body on fire for her. "There's nothing between us now. But I'll do no more than hold ye in my arms. Skin to skin. Heart to heart. And then I'm going to dress ye again. When I claim ye…and I give ye my sacred vow that I will…it will be as yer husband, and ye'll be my lawful wife."

She nodded. "You wouldn't be you, the proud, honorable Scot if you took me while I was betrothed to another."

"And ye could no' live with yerself if ye gave yerself to me and not yer husband. I would no' ask it of ye, nor will I take it from ye."

Her eyes were filled with love for him, for she did not hide anything of herself from him. "Robbie, you just promised me that you would be my husband. Do you mean it?"

"Aye, lass. But I dinna want to mislead ye. It might no' happen right away."

She pursed her lips, now regarding him with despair. "Are you saying we might be old and gray before we are ever together? Or perhaps not ever in this lifetime. Oh, Robbie. Do you believe in such things? That our hearts would recognize each other throughout time?"

"I dinna know. Lass, we still have another day to work on Tilbury. He's willing to try again with Melinda. All I need is for her to give him a ray of hope, and he'll release ye from the betrothal. We have a grand plan, one I canno' imagine she'll resist."

"Is this why you needed Dahlia?"

"Aye." He quickly told her what they intended to do tomorrow.

It was odd, holding her in his arms, both of them half undressed, and all they were doing was talking. He'd do more in a moment, of course. But Heather was not a one-night woman for him. She was the light in his heart, and he did not want her only for the pleasure of her body.

He wanted this. To hold her intimately. To talk to her, both of them trusting the other with their innermost feelings.

What they did not discuss is what he planned to do if Tilbury remained intent on marrying her. It did not bear mentioning. It might never come to that. No point in needlessly adding to her distress.

"If there's one thing I've learned when engaging in battle, it's never give up. Ye never know what can happen from one moment to the next."

"But we only have a day left, Robbie. How can we accomplish anything in so little time?"

"Some of the greatest battles in history have been fought and won in less than a day. Our battle isn't even underway yet. We're still negotiating. And Tilbury's no monster. He may hold out to the last, but I believe he will finally come around."

At least, it was his fervent hope.

Tilbury could not possibly be that much of a fool.

"No more talking, lass. I need to kiss ye." He kissed Heather on the lips before she had the chance to ask another question.

He ran his hands along her soft shoulders, splayed one across the small of her back. Cupped her cheek with his other. He needed to touch her.

Hold her.

But he also gave her the chance to touch him, to run her hands along his chest and tease her fingers in the dusting of gold hair across it. He watched as she poked and caressed the muscles of his arms and lightly kissed around the spot where he'd gotten the stitches on his wound. "It will leave a scar," she whispered.

"Aye, verra likely. But it serves a purpose."

She eyed him in confusion. "What purpose?"

He cast her a sloppy grin. "It will remind me not to be a drunken arse again."

She laughed. "You have other scars, but I expect those were earned in battle."

He nodded.

Now it was his turn to touch her and plant his mouth on her, to suckle and taste her sweet, warm skin.

"I have a scar, too," she said, suddenly breathless.

He eased his lips off the tip of her breast. "Where, lass. I dinna see it on ye." Not that his eyes were fixed anywhere but on her exquisite bosom.

"It's on my thigh."

Stars burst in his eyes. He knew what would happen if he reached down there to kiss and stroke her. His low brain would immediately and completely take over. He wouldn't stop at merely kissing the sweet inside of her leg. He'd soon have his mouth on her most intimate spot. Kissing her there. Licking her there. Taking her pearl into his mouth and suckling it.

Tasting her essence.

His body turned molten at the mere thought, his blood fiery and thick as it coursed through him. "I had better get ye dressed before this goes too far."

Even his voice was raspy and thick.

His hands shook as he drew her chemise over her breasts, for he wanted her so badly, and he was feeling the strain of denying himself the pleasure of her body.

"Must we?"

"Aye, lass. For now. I'll see ye tomorrow," he said, stepping away a moment to toss his shirt back on and shrug into his jacket. "My brain is about to explode. I need to get yer gown buttoned up again before I take if off ye completely and break my solemn vow."

"It amazes me, Robbie..." She did not resist as he raised her gown back over her shoulders and turned her so that he could fasten the buttons down her back.

He drew her hair aside to kiss her slender neck. "What does, love?"

"This. That you love me. I still cannot understand why."

He kissed her again on the delicate curve of her neck. "Why do ye love me? I'm an arrogant Scot with a bad reputation. Ye've seen me drunk and at my worst."

"I've never seen you drunk other than when you tumbled over the wall the other day." She laughed lightly. "I still wince whenever I think of it."

"Dinna tease me, lass. It was no' my finest moment."

"But I think you are a reformed rake, and everyone knows they make the best husbands. You are also intelligent, handsome, honorable, and brave. Best of all, you still have a little bit of the naughty in you to make you wicked fun. I shall always laugh with you, and my heart shall always be joyful whenever I'm around you. Now, your turn. Why me?"

He finished buttoning her gown and now turned her to face him. Her hair was still undone and spilling over her shoulders in lush waves. They'd have to search for the fallen pins, or else Romulus and Violet would know what he'd been doing to her.

"Why you?" He smiled at her and kissed her lightly on the tip of her nose. "Because ye are the sunshine in my life. I look at ye, and my heart is at ease. I look at ye, and I canno' help but smile. Ye make me happy. Ye feel good and right against my body." He groaned. "Too good just now. Let's find those pins I took out of yer hair, and then I

THE HEART OF LOVE

had better kiss ye goodnight and be on my way before I lose my resolve."

He knelt to feel along the carpet, and she did the same. "Pixie, do ye recall how many were in yer hair?"

She grinned. "Did you not count them as you were pulling them out?"

He chuckled. "I had other things on my mind, namely yer exquisite breasts."

"I thought you just said you loved me for my smile."

He arched an eyebrow wickedly. "Aye, lass. Yer smile and yer breasts. Dinna hit me. I canno' help wanting yer body, too."

"Yours is quite magnificent," she admitted. "Big and muscled. I was surprised by how good you felt against me even though there is nothing soft about your body. Yet, it felt divine. I think I had eight pins. I'm not sure. Does it matter?"

"Romulus will know what I did to ye if he finds even one on the floor. He'll feel that he failed in his duty to yer family. I dinna want him to feel badly about it."

She arched an eyebrow. "And you're not worried that he'll come after you for dishonoring me?"

"No. I'm sure he did the same to yer cousin. Only with honorable intentions, of course. He knew he wanted to marry her. It's our pawky low brain. It does no' ever shut off. Even after we've fixed our heart on the one lass we will love into eternity, that low brain keeps on working. But now, it only works on the lass we love." He continued to feel along the carpet. "I've found six."

Heather was kneeling beside him. "I've found two. I think that ought to do it."

He handed her the pins, then rose and drew her up with him. "I'll see ye tomorrow, lass."

She gave him a fierce hug. "And every day after that, I hope."

"Aye," he said, kissing her brow.

He tried not to sound concerned, but he was deeply worried about what tomorrow would bring. He wanted to resolve this peacefully, but all would fall apart if Melinda still resisted Tilbury.

Would Tilbury release Heather even if he did not have Melinda?

Perhaps Stoke could help him then, for he was no fool and had to know the marriage could not be allowed to take place. Better Stoke somehow stop it than him, for no one was going to jail a duke.

But Robbie knew that if all else failed, he'd ride off with Heather. He'd figure out a way to help her parents if Tilbury came after them. He could not bring himself to believe the man was that mean-spirited. But he would do all he could to protect her family if he sued them for Heather's breach of promise.

He stifled a sigh, wishing he could predict what tomorrow would bring.

CHAPTER THIRTEEN

HEATHER AWOKE EARLY the following morning and began to pace across her bedchamber like a lion trapped in a cage. But her pacing was not accomplishing anything other than wearing a hole in the new carpet Dahlia had helped Violet select. She paused to peer out the window, noting the drizzle still falling on the road and clinging to the leaves of trees in the garden and those that lined Chipping Way.

The sky was an unrelenting gray, and dark storm clouds moved swiftly against that gray backdrop, a harbinger of heavier rains to come.

The weather matched her dismal state of mind.

She was so worried about what would happen if Robbie did not succeed today. Another concern was her parents. Even if Tilbury did grant her the reprieve, there was no assurance her father would accept it. She was not yet of age to make her own decisions, and now that her parents were in town, her uncles, John and Rupert, no longer had the authority to act on their behalf.

She shook out of the thought.

Once she had Tilbury's release in writing, she would defy her parents and ride to Scotland with Robbie to legally marry him there. If he could not leave his position in London, she'd give herself to him right here...assuming his code of honor would allow him to compromise her in this fashion.

Last night, he'd gone so far as to take her clothes half off her. But taking her innocence outside of wedlock would be a huge step for him. She would have a struggle to convince him.

Not that she wished to be ruined.

She shook out of this thought as well.

"Mustn't worry," she muttered and resumed pacing because her skin was prickling, and she was too impatient to sit.

Robbie would be riding with Dahlia and Tilbury to the Camden Town flower stands about now. She hoped they would not be caught in a downpour. The flowers had to be delivered to Lady Melinda's home undamaged.

She glanced out the window again, wanting so badly to do something...anything. How could she stay put and do nothing to help herself? Yet, she did not wish to interfere with Robbie's plans. He was working hard to convince Tilbury to release her.

But was anyone working on Lady Melinda? After all, if she agreed to marry Tilbury, then all would be set right.

Tongues would wag, for those in the *ton* would find it highly amusing that Tilbury was desperately courting Lady Melinda even on the eve of his wedding. No one would feel any pity for her. After all, she was from a common Yorkshire family and would never be one of *them*. They would find it most amusing to learn Tilbury was Lady Melinda's mysterious marquess while she, the unworthy commoner, was merely a pale copy of this elegant duke's daughter.

Heather did not care that she would be made a laughingstock.

Indeed, she prayed for it.

By eleven o'clock in the morning, she was washed, dressed, had eaten her breakfast, and spent the last hour trying to read a book on ancient Greece in Romulus's library. She had the room to herself, for Romulus had left earlier today for a meeting at the Admiralty and was not expected to return before the end of the day.

But after reading the same page three times and still not knowing what it said, Heather shut the book and set it aside. She wandered into

THE HEART OF LOVE

Violet's sitting room and found her going over the daily menus with her housekeeper. Little Hyacinth was comfortably nestled in her arms and gurgling contentedly.

Innes had gone next door to play with Harry and Charles, who had been dropped off at their Aunt Sophie's house for the morning.

Violet cast her a heartbroken smile. "Come, sit a moment with me. Miss Mayhew and I are done going over the menus."

"I'll make up a list for the scullery maids to take to market," the efficient young woman said, bobbing her head to acknowledge Heather as she left.

Violet set aside her papers. "Are you all done packing your belongings?"

"No, I haven't started." Heather groaned. "It won't take long to accomplish. I'll have Agnes help me this evening if all else fails. But it won't. Robbie will find a way to change Tilbury's mind."

She leaned forward to watch Hyacinth sleeping so peacefully, her little lips twitching as she dreamt of feeding at her mother's breast. "You must be in heaven, Violet."

Her cousin laughed softly. "I am. Having Romulus home and both of us enjoying our new daughter is sheer bliss. He can only stay the week before he and Innes must return to Cornwall."

"It must be so hard on you."

"It is, especially at night when he is not here to hold me in his arms. But I would not ask him to give up the sea, nor would I ever wish for him to be anything other than the man he is. He's perfect."

Heather laughed. "He thinks you are perfect, too. I've never seen a man more besotted. You were so clever to both take *The Book of Love* to heart. I avoided reading it every which way I could. I've made every mistake possible. The worst part about it is now that I've read the book, I understand with such clarity who is the right man for me."

"Robbie MacLauren?"

"I knew it in my heart the moment I met him. But I was too stub-

145

born to let go of my little girl fantasy of marrying a marquess." She continued to watch Hyacinth as she slept. "I've now read the book several times over, and each time I do, I fall more deeply in love with him. All the things I thought were so important have faded to insignificance. The title, the trappings of wealth. I never had them, and I know I won't miss them."

"You now understand the richness that only true love can bring. I would have given up a king's ransom for Romulus. Not that anyone else wanted me."

"Violet, you would have had a line of suitors out the door had your heart not already been set on him. Speaking of hearts, I have something I must do. I cannot leave this matter of Tilbury and Lady Melinda all to Robbie to accomplish."

"What do you have in mind?"

Their conversation was cut short when Violet's maid knocked lightly at the door. "Miss Heather, you have a visitor."

She could not imagine who it was. "I do?"

The young woman nodded. "Lady Withnall has come to see you. I've settled her in the parlor."

"Oh." She hopped out of her chair. "Violet, may I have refreshments brought to the parlor for us?"

"Yes, of course. But I'll stay up here while you entertain her. You ought to see her alone. She would have asked for me if she had wanted to see me." She cast Heather a wry smile. "She and I are quite friendly. In truth, I credit her with matching me and Romulus. I think she's come here to help you along."

Heather laughed, knowing she and Violet were probably the only two people in London eager to see this feared gossip. Why hadn't she thought of inviting her sooner? After all, the woman knew everyone's secrets.

Heather had been so lost in her own thoughts, she hadn't heard the resounding *thuck, thuck, thuck* of the old harridan's cane along the polished entry hall floor. She hurried into the parlor. "Lady Withnall, I'm so happy to see you."

The older woman gave a cackling laugh. "That is something I rarely hear. But I had to come, my dear. Your love life is a mess, and there's no time to waste to set it right."

Heather sank onto the settee beside her. "I know. It's all my fault. You told me months ago that I'd already met the man who loves me. In my heart, I knew it was Captain MacLauren. But I've had this foolish dream ever since I was a little girl to marry a marquess. When Lord Tilbury came along, I didn't question his motives. I betrayed my own heart. And now we are in this impossible coil, and I'm not sure we can unravel it without someone getting hurt. I'm worried it will be my parents because I cannot go through with the wedding."

Lady Withnall patted her hand. "That's why I am here. Now, tell me. What were Tilbury, Captain MacLauren, and your sister, Dahlia, doing at the flower stands this morning?"

"You saw them?"

"Of course not. What would I be doing in Camden Town at that appallingly early hour of the morning? And in this weather, no less."

"Then how did you…? Never mind. I don't suppose it matters how you manage to uncover more secrets than all the elite agents of the Crown combined."

"I have my sources." She waved her hand in dismissal. "The flowers, Heather. What have they to do with you and Tilbury?"

Heather waited for the tea cart to be rolled in and left for them before responding. "Not with me. Captain MacLauren is trying to teach Tilbury how to properly woo Lady Melinda."

"It's about time. So, this is the reason for those flowers?"

"Yes. They're for her, not me. You know they care for each other…yes, of course you would know. I heartily approve of what Captain MacLauren is hoping to accomplish. But Tilbury's botched his courtship so badly, probably botched it for years now. Lady Melinda's hurt runs deep. I don't know the exact details of why they are at odds. Captain MacLauren did not confide in me all of what he learned."

"I should think not. That big Scot knows how to be discreet when it matters."

"Well, discreet or not, the problem remains. Tilbury will not release me from our betrothal unless he wins Lady Melinda's heart."

She poured Lady Withnall a cup of tea and offered her a slice of lemon cake.

"Lovely, I adore lemon cake. It suits my sour disposition," she said with a surprisingly kindly smile.

Was it possible Lady Withnall was going to help them?

Heather cleared her throat. "I know I am about to sound impertinent. But why are you here? Merely to gather more fodder for your gossip? Or do you think you can help us?" She poured a cup for herself as she spoke. "Because I think we are in desperate need of your wisdom and guidance. You tried to tell me to listen to my heart. I ignored the advice and regret it immeasurably."

"What Tilbury is doing to you is inexcusable." She took a sip of her tea. "I could forgive him for acting out of hurt, for he does love Lady Melinda. He's loved her ever since they were children."

"Was it the same for her? Has she always loved him?"

"Yes. There's a lovely honesty to children. They only learn to hide and manipulate once they are older. This is what both of them are doing now. I'm sure he behaved like a donkey, for all men do at some point or another. But he's been trying to make it up to her, and now she is the one behaving like a donkey."

"I think she's afraid to trust him with her love. She's afraid he will hurt her again."

Lady Withnall nodded. "Yes, that's it exactly."

"Captain MacLauren and Dahlia are helping him make a grand gesture, hoping to prove his love is true. They are buying as many flowers as they can find. But not just any, only those that signify love and faithfulness. He's also buying her a love token, a sapphire and diamond ring because sapphires represent true and faithful love. Captain MacLauren suggested adding the diamonds because they are meant to represent the sparkle Tilbury hopes to put back in Lady Melinda's eyes with his everlasting love."

"I always knew that big, handsome Scot had a romantic heart."

Heather set down her teacup. "I can see you like him. He's always had a way with the ladies, Lady Withnall."

"Is that your doubt surfacing?" She arched a thin, gray eyebrow.

"I suppose it is," Heather said, pursing her lips, "but only doubts about myself. Tilbury never wanted me. That's obvious now. And I know Captain MacLauren cares for me. I'm afraid one day he'll wake up and realize he's made a mistake. Is it possible for me to hold such a man forever?"

"You are looking at it backward, my dear." She reached over and patted her hand. "The man has had women tossing themselves at him ever since he was a lad, yet not one of them ever held his heart. Then you came along, and he knew instantly. Not only will you hold his heart forever, but you will be the only one ever with the power to break it."

The notion shocked Heather, and yet, wasn't this the same way she felt about him? "There is no other man for me. I cannot marry Tilbury, but he has threatened to crush my family if I renege on our betrothal. Captain MacLauren and I are not cheats. If I marry Lord Tilbury, I will be honor-bound to hold to my marriage vows. Nor will Captain MacLauren ever lure me into straying because of that Scottish code of honor of his."

She clasped her hands together, holding them tightly as she struggled against her tears. She did not want to turn into a watering pot. Tears solved nothing. "I hope Tilbury and Lady Melinda find happiness, I truly do. But even if they do not, this game Tilbury is playing has to end. He will destroy all of our lives. How can he not see this? Is there anything you can do?"

Lady Withnall patted her hand. "This is why I am here, my dear. Stoke is having a few of us over this afternoon. We regularly get together for card games, mostly whist, which is something we elders enjoy playing. You will come with me."

Heather leaped at the chance. "I'd love to. Do you think the duke will allow me in? Captain MacLauren is doing his best with Tilbury, but that leaves no one working on Lady Melinda. I was thinking of going over there unannounced later today if Robbie's...I mean, Captain MacLauren's ploy did not work. Going over there with you is a wonderful idea."

"I know. That is why I suggested it. While Captain MacLauren's idea has merit, it may not be enough. Tilbury is now willing, but Melinda is not. She is still acting out over her mother's death. They had a very close relationship, and losing her was very hard on the girl. Then Tilbury broke her heart when she was at her most vulnerable, and she has not recovered from it yet. She gave him all of her heart, all of herself. He treated this gift like it was nothing. This is why she has trouble trusting him now."

"Does she still love him?"

"Oh, yes. True love never dies. Trusting him is her concern. This is what he must convince her to do. I'm not certain how one does that when there is so little time."

Heather's heart sank. "It would take a leap of faith."

"Yes, and we must help her make that leap." She rapped her cane on the carpet and rose. "Change out of your morning gown and put on suitable attire for an afternoon party. I'll be waiting in my carriage."

"Surely, that cannot be comfortable for you. Violet will come down and—"

"No need to disturb your cousin when she's busy with her new baby. I'll pay a call on her and little Hyacinth another day. Hurry along. Meet me in my carriage. There's no time to lose."

Heather hugged the little termagant. "Thank you. No matter the outcome. Thank you."

She raced upstairs.

Violet had set Hyacinth in the cradle for her nap and followed Heather into her bedchamber. "What are you doing? Is Lady Withnall still here? I had better go down to greet her."

"No, she'll visit you another day. She has already returned to her carriage. I need your help. What shall I wear?"

"Not this one," she said, pointing to the robin's egg blue silk that was meant to be her wedding gown…assuming a wedding would take place tomorrow. She desperately hoped to have no use for it. "How about this one? The pale rose is lovely. Here, let me help you with your buttons. Good, now slip this rose one on." Violet took a step back. "Let me see your hair. Did my maid help you style it this morning?"

Heather nodded.

"It looks very nice. Here, let me do up the last buttons. Where is your reticule? And the matching gloves? Oh, let me see your shoes. Here, wear these. They're daintier." She helped Heather put them on. "You look beautiful. Now, out you go." She turned her around and shoved her out the door.

Heather raced downstairs. "Grieves, I'm in a hurry!"

She'd annoyed the poor man all morning long, continually opening the door to poke her head out of it as though something miraculous would be standing on the other side to greet her.

Grieves hopped to the task, opening the door and smiling as she tore out.

Her cheeks were hot, and she was breathing heavily by the time she hopped into Lady Withnall's carriage. "I hope I did not keep you waiting too long."

"Not at all, my dear. Now take several deep breaths and calm yourself. We have our work cut out for us. And do not fling yourself across the seat to hug me again, or I shall toss you out of the carriage and take myself home."

Heather laughed. "Then, I shall use only words to convey my gratitude to you."

"I'll have my thanks when I see you properly married to that handsome Scot." Lady Withnall cast one of her rare smiles.

Heather grinned back, but she turned thoughtful a moment later. "May we speak about Captain MacLauren again?"

"Yes, my dear."

"We mentioned taking a leap of faith before. You seem so certain Captain MacLauren will never hurt me. But his reputation with the ladies still nags at the back of my mind. He's known as a cad and a hound. What makes you so confident he won't tire of me one day and return to his old ways?"

She arched a gray eyebrow. "What I think doesn't matter. Why do you believe in him? I can see that he has your trust."

"He does. I'm not sure exactly why, but it's something I feel deep in my soul. He's honorable. He would never lie to me. He has pledged to be faithful." She shook her head and sighed. "It's his Scottish pride, I think. He lives by a code of honor. When he gives his oath, he will keep it to the end. And yet, if Tilbury had said the same to me, I don't know that I would have believed him. Perhaps it is that I know Captain MacLauren would unhesitatingly risk his life to save me. Lord Tilbury would think about it first."

"Then let's hope Tilbury feels the same way about Melinda as MacLauren feels about you. This is what it will take to convince her."

"We're not going to put her life in danger, are we?"

Lady Withnall sniffed indignantly. "Of course not. It would be disastrous if he failed the test. I like Tilbury, mind you. But he isn't like your handsome Scot. He's used to people protecting him, not the other way around. He does not have the instincts of a soldier, but those of a politician. He is a creature of the House of Lords. We are most definitely not putting his instincts, decent though they may be, to the test."

They rode quietly the rest of the way and soon reached the Duke of Stoke's magnificent residence. "My sister, Dahlia, helped them decorate it. She's wonderfully talented. I wonder if they'll now tear down everything she did because they have no more use for my family."

"The Upper Crust can be petty. Oh, look at all the carriages lined up. I believe everyone in our club has shown up. No doubt, word has spread about Tilbury buying out the flower carts and having the flowers delivered to Melinda instead of you. They are all here to view the spectacle."

"Oh, crumpets."

Lady Withnall patted her hand. "Be ready to be mocked, my dear. I'm sorry, but many of them will view you as the unworthy rustic, the outsider who got what she deserved. Not that they're worthy of anything themselves. This is why I revel in exposing their dirty secrets. They need to be taken down a peg."

Heather nodded. "I'm ready for it. I don't care if they laugh in my face. It will be nothing if Tilbury finally agrees to let me out of the betrothal."

They waited in the queue with the other carriages, watching as delivery carts laden with flowers passed them by to drive around back to the servants' entrance. As they slowly moved up, Heather worried that perhaps she ought to have stayed home with Violet.

She dismissed the twinge of doubt, for Lady Withnall was never wrong and wouldn't have escorted her here if she thought it was a mistake.

The Stoke butler announced them. "Lady Withnall and Miss Heather Farthingale."

She hadn't expected her name to resound through the duke's magnificent music room or to have a room full of his card-playing friends gawking at her. There were about thirty ladies and gentlemen present, including the duke and Lady Melinda. The room had been set up with card tables. The pianoforte had been pushed to a corner, while along a back wall, more tables had been set up to accommodate a sumptuous light repast.

Everyone fell to a hush the moment her name was announced.

Heather's heart shot into her throat, and she briefly considered running away, but Lady Withnall had latched onto her arm with a steel grip and was not about to let her flee. It was unnecessary. She was not going to budge from here until the matter was settled.

She had matured quite a bit over the past few days, ever since Robbie's return to London. All the excuses she had made up for herself, all the reasons why she should choose Tilbury over Robbie, had fallen by the wayside. What remained was the knowledge that whatever hardships she and Robbie had to face, they'd overcome them together. Whatever compromises one of them had to make for the other, they would make them.

"Stoke," Lady Withnall said with a resounding *thuck* of her cane on his exquisitely polished wood floor, "I hear your study has been redecorated. You and your daughter must give me and Miss Farthingale a private tour. Now, if you please."

The tiny harridan then cast a warning glance to encompass all his well-heeled guests. Their smirks faded, and they suddenly looked like wayward children who had just been sternly rapped across the knuckles.

As for the duke, he looked so angry, one could imagine steam spouting out of his ears. "What is the meaning of this?"

Lady Withnall ignored the question, instead turning her back on him and walking toward his study. "Come, Stoke. You, too, Melinda."

To Heather's surprise, they gave no further protest, and meekly followed them into the duke's study.

But Stoke rounded on Lady Withnall the moment the door was

closed behind them. "What in blazes is Tilbury's betrothed doing here? Must she further humiliate my daughter? Isn't it enough she's got Tilbury?"

Lady Withnall nodded to her. "Go ahead, my dear. Set the duke straight."

Heather hadn't expected to be the one to do the talking, but she was not about to let the opportunity pass. "I don't have Lord Tilbury. He loves Lady Melinda. Is it not obvious why he offered for me? You have only to look at us side by side to know the reason why. She rejected his proposal, and so he proposed to me out of spite. Now, he will not let me out of the betrothal unless your daughter agrees to marry him."

Melinda frowned at her. "Why should I do that? He's shown himself to be inconsiderate and inconstant."

"I agree about the inconsiderate part. What he did was supremely foolish and hurtful to both of us. But he isn't inconstant. The one constant in all this has been that he loves you. He has always loved you. He will always love you. There is no room in his heart for anyone else. But he does not know how to properly show it."

Melinda's expression softened, but only the littlest bit. "Is this why flowers by the wagon load have been arriving here all morning? Is this his way of making amends?"

Heather nodded. "He's desperate to have you."

They stared at her, the duke now openly scowling. "Is this supposed to endear him to my daughter and me? What am I to think of a man who would openly court my daughter when he has promised to marry you tomorrow?"

"Very little, I suppose. But I am desperate to be released from our betrothal, and he will not do it unless he knows he has won Lady Melinda's hand and her heart. Please, give him this chance. I don't love him. He doesn't love me. He never did. He never will. He proposed to me because I resemble you, Lady Melinda. Surely, you must have noticed."

Melinda gave a slight nod.

"The thing is, if you love him, then give him this chance. Forgive me if I speak out of turn, but I think you do love him and always have. You must be in terrible pain right now, for how does one ever stop caring for one's true love? But we are now at the point of no return. You know this. Will you not seize your chance at happiness?"

"Miss Farthingale," the duke said, "if you are so desperate to get out of the betrothal, then why did you not simply break it off with him? What hold does he have on you that you cannot simply walk away?"

"He has threatened to sue my family if I call it off. He will crush them, leave them with nothing. I cannot let it happen. I don't know if he is serious. I did not think he had it in him to be so cruel, but I cannot risk that he is. We don't have the wealth or connections to fight back."

"If he would behave this way with you, then why should I give him a second chance?" Lady Melinda asked. "What makes you think he would treat me any better?"

Heather was making a mess of pleading her case. If anything, she was reinforcing Lady Melinda's reasons for refusing him again. "Everything he has done has been to gain your attention. You are his world. He needs lessons in how to properly show you how he feels."

Lady Withnall snorted. "Obviously. The man is an utter dolt in matters of love. Pathetic and incompetent."

Heather wasn't certain the comment helped her case. "I think he's coming around to realizing that marriage takes compromise and consideration, that love is not a business negotiation where one must always maintain the upper hand and bluff one's opponent. This is his error. Until now, he has never viewed a wife as a partner, but as an opponent."

The duke did not appear convinced. "Well, he's realized it too late."

Heather shook her head. "It isn't too late. But it will be by tomorrow unless he agrees to release me, which I doubt he will do if nothing changes. He and I shall be unhappily married." Well, she wasn't going to marry him, but they did not have to know it yet. She turned to Melinda. "You will also be unhappy because you still love him. He will not be your husband. He will not have children with you. Your Grace, will you not ache to see your daughter alone and miserable?"

The duke growled softly. "Enough, Miss Farthingale. You have made your point."

She nodded, for there was nothing more she could say. "Thank you for your time, Your Grace. And for yours, Lady Melinda."

She was about to leave when Melinda spoke up. "Are you blaming me for this situation, Miss Farthingale?"

The question surprised her. "Not at all. If anything, I am to blame. I was so caught up in marrying a title that I ignored all the warning signs as well as the urging of my heart. Farthingales marry for love, so rather than listen to what my heart was telling me, I convinced myself that I could fall in love with Lord Tilbury and never bothered to question why he would want me in the first place. A foolish mistake on my part. I've ruined four lives because of it."

The duke's demeanor softened. "Well, it is Tilbury who would be responsible for ruining your life and that of my daughter. You are trying to rectify your mistake, and he won't let you."

Heather nodded reluctantly.

The more they spoke, the more the marquess was made to appear the ogre in all this. She wouldn't blame Melinda for refusing his suit. Indeed, she could not imagine Robbie ever behaving so unchivalrously. "I had better go. Thank you again for your time."

"No, Miss Farthingale," the duke said. "Stay. It seems you are the opening act in this theater of the absurd. How soon before Tilbury makes his appearance?"

"That I do not know, but I expect it will be soon. It is best if I were not here when he arrives."

"On the contrary," the duke said. "I think you ought to take a seat beside my daughter. What will he say when he sees the two of you together as he attempts to propose to my Melinda?" He must have thought the notion hilarious because he burst out laughing. "Ah, that will be priceless."

Heather thought it was a dreadful idea. "No, Your Grace. That will be hurtful to your daughter."

As for herself, she no longer cared how thorough her own humiliation would be. She just wanted to be in Robbie's arms and free to marry him.

Lady Melinda took her hand and tucked it in the crook of her arm. "My father's idea has merit. What do you say, Miss Farthingale? Shall we sit together and wait for our Tilbury to show his face?"

"As I said, I think it is a terrible idea. I ought to go." Heather glanced at Lady Withnall, hoping for a word of support, but the woman was now studying the wallpaper and muttering compliments on Dahlia's work, completely ignoring the conversation.

"I think I shall ask her to redecorate my house when she's finished with yours, Stoke. It is as old and musty as I am, and definitely in need of refurbishing."

She turned to Heather and noticed that her arm was tucked in Melinda's. "Ah, Stoke. Escort me into the card room. This will be better than opening night at the theater. Too bad I did not think to bring my lorgnette. Now I shall have to squint as the spectacle unfolds."

The others were now eager for Tilbury's arrival, but Heather was not.

What would he say?

What would he do?

How badly was he going to humiliate her?

Not that she cared.

However, he was an extremely prideful man.

How badly were they going to humiliate him?

CHAPTER FOURTEEN

R OBBIE HAD SPENT the entire morning with Tilbury, propping up this marquess who was now a jumble of fears and doubts, and distraught enough to give up on winning Lady Melinda's hand in marriage. The wretched man was not likely to gain favor with her if he showed up babbling whatever popped in his head and then unceremoniously casting up his accounts.

"Bollocks," Robbie muttered to himself, for they were now out of time, and Tilbury had no other choice but to make a jackass of himself before the woman he loved and what was likely to be a crowd of onlookers if the carriages lined up across the street were any indication.

Tilbury, he was coming to realize, did not know the first thing about courtship or romance. Indeed, he had absolutely no romantic instincts. But he had a deep and abiding love for Melinda. If only he hadn't ruined it beyond repair.

Tilbury's eyes suddenly rounded in terror as they stood at the Duke of Stoke's front door. "MacLauren, I forgot completely!"

Robbie groaned. "What now?"

"This is Stoke's card day. He will have a houseful of card-playing friends with him." He turned to run, but Robbie grabbed him and held him back.

"All the better," he said, his own stomach churning. "The gesture is even grander when made in front of others."

Blessed saints.

Could anything else go wrong?

He tried to calm Tilbury as the butler opened the door to them. The man's gaze was as cold as a glacier. "Lord Tilbury?"

Obviously, he had not been expected.

Since Tilbury looked as though he was not breathing, Robbie responded. "Aye, Lord Tilbury and Captain Robert MacLauren to see His Grace and Lady Melinda."

The butler nodded. "I shall see if His Grace is at home."

Robbie returned to bolstering Tilbury's resolve. "Ye've been playing a cowardly game for months now, unwittingly making a fool of yer beloved. Ye have to do this. Take a deep breath. Muster yer courage."

"How have I made a fool of Melinda? She's the one who has given me a hard time."

Robbie kept a hand clamped on Tilbury's shoulder. "Dinna we go over this on the ride over? If ye keep up this attitude, she's going to boot ye out of the house. What will it accomplish? She'll spend the next thirty years alone and crying in her bed."

"What about me?"

"This is no' about ye. Not today. Ye are to think only of Lady Melinda. Ye pledged yer heart to another, and in doing so, ye broke her heart. Can ye not understand the enormity of what ye did to hurt her?"

He gave the marquess a nudge forward as Stoke's butler approached. "Ye're now going to make a monumental arse of yerself because this is the only way to put the two of ye on even footing again. Then ye're going to release Heather and get down on bended knee to propose to Melinda."

Stoke's butler stared at both of them with disdain. "His Grace will see you now." He turned to escort them to the duke.

Tilbury hesitated. "Are you certain you're not setting me up for humiliation because you want Heather for yourself, and I won't allow it?"

"Ye've set yerself up for this mockery because of yer idjit actions. Aye, I want Heather. Ye want Lady Melinda. Ye've set out the terms. I'll only get Heather if ye get Melinda. Frankly, yer determination to hold on to Heather is making my skin crawl."

"Now see here! What else was I supposed to do?"

"Seriously? I don't have time to make a list of all the reasons this is wrong. For one, she is no' yer beloved. She will never be a proper replacement for yer beloved. So ye're going to do whatever it takes to make Melinda accept ye. Take a deep breath. Now, go in there and make a braying arse of yerself."

Robbie's heart sank to his toes when he realized they were being led to the duke's music room and not his private quarters. *Bollocks.* This was going to be a bloodbath.

He grimaced as the butler announced Tilbury to the guests. He was also announced, but no one cared about him. Anyway, he was not going to step into the room. He intended to stand in the doorway to block the marquess if he tried to run.

He prayed as he'd never prayed in his life for a miracle to happen.

Then he glanced in the room and saw who was seated beside Melinda.

Heather!

Lord, is this yer idea of a jest? Because I dinna find it funny.

What was he going to do now?

More importantly, what was Tilbury going to do?

In all their discussions. In all their planning. They hadn't considered this.

Of course, this was Lady Withnall's meddling hand. She was seated beside Heather, smirking at him and Tilbury.

He had told Heather to stay out of it, and this little harridan had dragged her straight into the circle of fire.

Tilbury stood there, speechless.

Well, at least he was not running.

The room was as quiet as a tomb. No one moved. No one breathed.

Lady Melinda's eyes took on a translucent gleam. Och, it was no' the gleam of love. No, it was predatory. It was the look in the eyes of a lioness about to pounce on her unwitting prey and eat him alive. "Lord Tilbury, what a pleasant surprise. And now we are all here together. You, me, and your betrothed. What a jolly party we shall have."

Tilbury ran a hand through his hair.

Still speechless.

"Is there something you wish to say to me? Surely, it can be said in front of your betrothed. The two of you can have no secrets from each other."

"No…no…it's too cruel," he muttered.

Robbie wasn't sure what the marquess meant by the remark. Too cruel for Heather to hear his love declaration to Melinda? Too cruel for him to be played the fool by the two women in his life?

To Robbie's way of thinking, Tilbury was getting what he deserved. All of this could have been avoided simply by releasing Heather. But he wouldn't let her go. He was the one cruelly manipulating both ladies and solely responsible for exacerbating the problem. They were now giving him back a little of his own.

Melinda still had the look of a lioness on the prowl. "Oh, and thank you for the lovely flowers you've been sending all day. They are from you, are they not?"

Robbie was afraid Tilbury's heart would simply rupture, and he'd fall dead on the floor. Well, if he was dead, he couldn't marry Heather. That would fix the problem.

He doubted they would have such luck.

Tilbury's face was ashen. He looked as though he was about to faint. Robbie strode to his side, wishing he could just let the bloody fool fall on his face. But his blasted Scottish pride would not allow him to stand by and let the man be injured.

Tilbury waved him back. "No, MacLauren. We are done here." He reached into his pocket and took out the box that held the sapphire ring. He handed it to Melinda. "Open it later. Something to remember me by. The sapphire represents faithfulness and constancy." He glanced at Robbie. "Isn't that right, MacLauren?"

"Aye, my lord."

Oh, hell. Hell. Hell.

"The diamonds represent the way your eyes used to sparkle whenever you looked at me. I haven't seen that beautiful sparkle in your eyes in a long time. And I ached, knowing I had destroyed it and could not put it back. I tried, but you did not trust me enough. All I ever wanted was to make you happy. Keep the ring. It's yours to do with as you wish. Those gems will survive a thousand years, well beyond our existence. Toss it away. Lock it away. Or put it on and never take it off. I can no longer bear to think of it or you. I'm done. My heart cannot withstand the burden of pain any longer."

Robbie silently recalled every Gaelic curse known to exist in the history of mankind.

This wasn't happening.

This couldn't be happening.

Tilbury turned to Heather. "I am truly sorry, my dear. I never meant to hurt you. And I shall do my best to be a good husband to you."

Heather leaped to her feet. "What? No!"

"The sort of husband I would have been to Melinda if she'd given me the chance. You are not released. I shall see you at St. Mary's tomorrow." He stormed out.

Robbie could have stopped him, but he merely stepped aside to let him pass. Tilbury had made his grand gesture. He'd humiliated himself thoroughly, and it had all been for naught. Now he and Heather had to plan their next step.

Stoke looked worried.

Melinda was now in tears.

Heather was in tears.

The guests were now out of their chairs and all clamoring to talk at once. That is, all of them were up and buzzing save Lady Withnall, who was still seated and calmly sipping a lemonade.

Would any judge convict him of strangling the little harpy? Why did she have to bring Heather here?

He strode to Heather's side, not certain what to do or say. To his mind, this wasn't over yet. It would not be over until Heather exchanged vows with Tilbury tomorrow morning. They had options. He could ride off to Scotland with her right now.

He was ready to ride off with her at any point before the ceremony took place. He'd ride Gallant into the church, if necessary.

He did not take Heather into his arms since he wasn't sure how she would respond. But he eased when she came to him on instinct, for he was the one she would turn to whenever troubled. "Och, lass. We'll move to the next plan. It is no' over yet."

"Robbie, he openly courted another woman in front of me. Is this not grounds to break off the betrothal? Surely, it must be."

"The law does not work fairly, lass. Had ye done this to him, there would be no question. But he's a marquess, and ye're a merchant's daughter. Even if they thought ye'd been wronged, they would no' go against Tilbury if he demanded the betrothal be upheld."

"So, there is still no way out for me without risking the ruination of my parents? This is my fault again. I've made things worse, not better. I shouldn't have been here. I only meant to talk privately with His Grace and Lady Melinda. Then you and Tilbury arrived and..."

Stoke approached him. "So, this was your brilliant idea, MacLau--ren?"

"Aye, I'll take full responsibility for it. But I dinna make Lord Tilbury utter a word he did not mean. He loves yer daughter. Will ye just stand there and glower at me, or are ye going to do something about it? We are down to mere hours now to fix this." He glanced at Melinda, who was still in tears as she opened the box and withdrew the ring with shaking hands.

At least she hadn't yet tossed it across the room.

He and the duke watched as she slid it onto her finger. She kept it on and stood staring down at her hand through her veil of tears.

Lady Withnall finally rose and came toward him. "I suppose Tilbury's taken himself off and left you behind. Ride back to Chipping Way with me and Heather. There's nothing more you can do here."

He spared a glance at Stoke. "Fight for yer daughter's happiness."

He kept his arm around Heather as he led her out of the duke's residence, quite aware of Lady Withnall walking beside them. "Why did ye bring Heather here?"

The termagant did not appear at all remorseful. "Melinda and her father needed to hear the plea from her. You were too busy worrying about Tilbury to think about Melinda. But she needed a talking to as well. So did her father."

"How did it go?"

"Heather spoke from her heart. She was honest and brilliant."

Despite his irritation, he smiled. "Och, I dinna doubt it. The lass does no' lie."

"Except to herself," Lady Withnall remarked.

"Aye." He assisted Lady Withnall into her carriage and then gave a hand up to Heather. He climbed in last and settled beside the lass who had claimed his heart. "I'm willing to take her up to Scotland, ride out today if she'll agree to it."

"Robbie, I won't do it. I cannot risk Tilbury suing my parents. He'll do it, too. You saw the stubborn set to his jaw. He still won't let me go, you've just confirmed as much. All is lost to him, and it has done nothing to sway his mind. He thinks he can recreate the woman of his dreams by marrying me."

They rode in silence for several minutes before Heather turned to Lady Withnall. "Do you think the minister will allow me to deliver a speech?"

The older woman was smiling broadly now. "Don't ask him for permission, just do it. It's your ceremony. You can say whatever it is you wish to say. What do you have in mind?"

"I'm not sure of the exact words yet, but it will be an appeal of the heart. Surely, if Tilbury loves Lady Melinda, he has to know he cannot go through with marrying me, or he'll lose her forever. He has to know that if he forces me to marry him, then how can I ever honor him? How can he ever know happiness when he and I will be the most miserable couple ever to marry?"

"Och, lass. I dinna think any of it will sink into his thick head if it hasn't sunk in by now. Nor would I want ye to make war with yer husband. If ye will no' ride to Scotland with me, then I'd want ye to be happy in yer marriage. I'd never wish sadness on ye."

She curled against his arm. "It's too late, Robbie. My heart will never heal from losing you."

"Nor will mine ever heal, lass."

"You could abduct him, MacLauren. Keep him away from the ceremony," Lady Withnall suggested.

"I've already considered it," he said with a nod. "But it won't stop him from suing Heather's family. It will land me in prison. And he keeps too many footmen close at hand. I canno' take them all on."

"It isn't too late to kill him."

Robbie rolled his eyes. "I dinna kill in cold blood, Lady Withnall. But I did briefly consider it as well. No, either Heather rides to Scotland with me or…"

"Can you not say it? Either she's with you for Scotland, or she marries Tilbury." The older woman studied him with her beady eyes.

"Unless he has a change of heart."

"Which he'll no' have, but we can always pray for a miracle." He leaned forward. "Would ye mind dropping us at Joshua and Holly's house? Heather may as well let her family know what's happened."

"Of course." She thumped her cane on the roof and gave her driver the new direction.

"Oh, good heavens. My parents will throw a fit when I tell them what went on today. It pains me to say this, but they will be delighted I'm still stuck with the marquess."

Lady Withnall grunted. "They are social climbers, as are many parents. It is nothing new."

Heather nodded. "Will you join us? I'm sure Holly will be pleased for your company."

She cackled. "No, my dear. I shall drop you off, then be on my way. I'll see you at St. Mary's tomorrow."

"Unless I take her to Scotland," Robbie intoned.

"As I said, I shall see you tomorrow. You won't carry her off to Gretna Green because it would put her parents in harm's way, and you would not take her against her will. Are you certain you will not reconsider killing Tilbury?" She sighed. "No, I suppose you wouldn't."

The carriage drew up in front of Joshua and Holly's residence soon after. Robbie was about to help Heather down when the lass turned to Lady Withnall and gave her a fierce hug. "I know this irritates you, but I don't care. Thank you for helping me out. At least I got to speak to Lady Melinda and her father. Not that it did any good, but at least we tried."

"Girl, you are impossible! Save your hugs for your big, handsome Scot."

Robbie frowned. "I will no' be—"

"Save your piety, MacLauren. True love cannot be denied. That is all I'll say on the matter. Would you care to place a wager on the wedding taking place?"

He scowled at her.

"Too bad. I wonder if the local bookmakers are taking bets on you yet." She thumped on her roof again. "Scranton, take me to the Strand bookmakers. This ought to be interesting."

Robbie kept a light hold on Heather after helping her down from the carriage. They stood together and watched until the elegant conveyance disappeared around the corner. "Do you think she'll bet for us or against us, Robbie?"

He arched an eyebrow. "Pixie, she believes in true love. For us, of course. She'll wager her house that no wedding will take place. And it is time for ye to consider this seriously. There is a risk if ye break it off with Tilbury that he will sue yer family. But there's also a chance he won't pursue his claim, or if he does, that the judge would rule against him."

"How much of a chance of a ruling in our favor do you think?"

He grimaced. "Slim to none, if ye're asking my honest opinion. And yet, I cannot believe he would push it that far. This is a side of him I've not seen before. I've had a year's dealing with him in my position as military liaison and have not known him to be vindictive."

"That's business. This is as personal as a thing can be."

"Aye, lass. I know. But I dinna think a man's nature can be so at odds."

"If only it were true. Perhaps a cornice stone will fall on his head and bring him back to his senses. Do you think he might back down at the final hour?" Heather regarded him with hope in her eyes but also a mix of trepidation.

"I canno' say for certain. What I do know is that yer worth to him is as his hostage. The game is over once he takes you as his wife. There's no play to be had after you exchange vows."

She nodded. "This is how I feel, like a hostage and not a bride."

"We've tried to make him see reason, but it's time to make our own plans. He canno' control this game. I won't let him. Let's sort through the possibilities and the consequences. If the threat to ruin yer family does no' work to hold ye, then he gains nothing by pursuing a legal action other than the cruel pleasure of exacting revenge on a helpless family."

"Isn't that enough?"

"Once ye are married to me, you will no' be entirely at his mercy. Ye'll have the clans of Scotland behind ye if he attempts to give yer family trouble. Caithness for certain. Probably Hume, since my cousin, Thad, is heir to the Earl of Hume. Ye would not be powerless."

"I'm sure my Farthingale relations would also come to my aid."

He nodded reluctantly. "Aye, but I dinna like to get them involved. They live in London, as does Tilbury, and must deal with each other socially and professionally. Ye dinna want these peers taking sides and brawling in the House of Lords."

"How would it be different with only the Scottish lords involved?"

"Och, lass. We Scots live for a good fight, especially against the Sassenachs. We dinna like them, and they dinna like us. We are piss on their boots. But we Scots will no' be threatened. We know how to fight back."

"I see. Fight back? You aren't going to do anything foolish when you leave here, are you?"

"Depends."

"On what?"

He cast her a devilish but gorgeous smile. "On yer definition of foolish."

Chapter Fifteen

"ROBBIE, LET'S TAKE a walk around the square first. I need a little more time to think before I face my parents." Heather dreaded the possibility of having to talk to them just yet. However, there was little chance of avoiding them and not only because they had settled in with Holly and Joshua. They deserved to be told what was happening since they were the ones who stood to lose everything by her actions.

There were mere hours left, less than twenty, before everyone headed off to St. Mary's Church and the dreaded ceremony in the morning.

"Still hoping for a miracle, lass?"

She nodded as he tucked her arm in his, and they began to stroll. "As you said, it isn't over until Tilbury and I exchange vows. Oh, Robbie. I don't know if I can form the words. *I do.* I think my heart will burst if I have to say them."

"Then don't say them, Heather. We'll deal with the consequences as they arise, assuming there are any."

"I hate that we are caught up in Tilbury's game. And what of Lady Melinda? She's played plenty of games of her own. I hate that we've been dragged in. I don't think I shall sleep at all tonight. I'll just stay on my knees and pray until daylight breaks, and then I'll pray some more."

"Fretting and agonizing will accomplish nothing. Get a good

night's rest, lass. Ye'll need it."

She laughed mirthlessly. "Why? Are we going to make a run for it?"

He shrugged. "If ye wish. Ye have only to say the word, and I'll take ye up to Scotland."

"They'll put you in prison. I'm not putting you in harm's way."

"Do I no' have a say in the matter?"

She sighed. "Walking isn't helping much to clear my mind. Dahlia and Holly will be waiting for me, I'm sure. You said that you and Tilbury dropped Dahlia here before going on to visit Stoke. I might as well let her know the plan was a disaster."

"It wasn't. Ye dinna know that for certain. Good things happened as well. The pair finally confronted each other. Stoke is now aware of all that's been going on between Tilbury and his daughter. He may have suspected, but I'm sure he was surprised by some of what was said. She put on his damn ring. It has to mean something."

"I hope so. This is so frustrating, Robbie."

He arched a golden eyebrow, looking quite handsome as a sliver of sunlight broke through the clouds and shone down on him. Of course, it would. This was Robbie, and the sun couldn't help but shine on him. "Lass, just remember, this game is not in their control. Aye, we have indulged them in the hope of a peaceful reconciliation. But in fact, the outcome is entirely in your hands. There may be consequences. I'm willing to suffer whatever may fall upon me. But I will no' force ye to do anything ye dinna wish to do."

He glanced around and saw that no one was on the street, so he led her into the small park in the center of the square and kissed her behind one of the lush trees. The kiss was gentle and soft, yet there was a smolder in his gaze. "I'll be at the church for the ceremony. Ye have only to say the word, and I'll take ye away. Gallant will enjoy a good run."

She tugged him closer, enjoying the feel of his body against hers and the musk scent of his skin. "Tell me about your Highlands, Robbie. Why do you love it so much?"

He kissed her brow. "It is a glorious place. A rugged land of hills and glens and soaring peaks. Ye can hear the sea batter the coast from miles inland. Ye can hear the whistle of the wind as it blows across the hills and through the fields of heather. There is no finer sight than a hawk soaring above a mountain valley, its wings outstretched against the bluest sky ye've ever beheld."

She closed her eyes and tried to imagine what he was describing.

"The water in the lochs and rivers is the color of blue ice. It's cold enough to shrivel a man's bollocks. Sorry, lass. But this is what we Scots do. Fight the cold. Fight nature. But we also respect it. There are faerie pools and waterfalls hidden within the glens that will be more to yer comfort, for the sun warms those waters. I'll take ye to one of those faerie glens once we're married."

She smiled while listening to him.

"The lore says if the faeries come upon a couple truly in love, they'll bless them with beautiful children."

"And if the couple is not in love?"

He grinned. "They'll send the wife's mother to live with them."

Heather laughed. "You are making it all up."

He held up his hands in mock surrender. "It's all true. My brother, Malcolm, will confirm it. He and his wife have been popping children out so fast, they'll need to add another wing onto the castle just to accommodate them."

"The castle?"

"Aye, lass. We have castles in Caithness. Where do ye think the Earl of Caithness and his family would live?"

She nibbled her lip and fretted. "Would we live there, Robbie?"

"Aye. My granduncle is earl, and Dornoch Castle is his. Malcolm will inherit it along with the title eventually, so he's there with Anne and their children. Malcolm and I call our granduncle our grandda because he raised us, and he likes to have us all under his roof. He has been more of a grandfather, even a father, to us than our own."

"He sounds like a wonderful man."

"Aye, but he can also be hardheaded and stubborn. Meddlesome, too. If ye wish for more privacy, we could settle at Brora Castle. It is another of his castles, and I know he would no' mind. They aren't grand like the English castles. Just big piles of weathered, gray stone, and drafty whenever it turns cold or rainy…and it is often cold or rainy. 'Tis a hard land for farming, too. A man can break his back trying to make something grow out of the stubborn soil. But we are never far from the sea, and the fish are always plentiful."

"It sounds wonderful."

They returned to Holly's house, and Heather's thoughts turned to her parents. Perhaps the mention of living in a castle, no matter how old and dank it was, might convince them to allow her to marry Robbie.

Not that they would agree to it straight away, even if Tilbury was no longer a threat to them. They were snobs and wanted *better* for her. To them, it was all about rank and prominence in London society. Marrying a soldier and living in a remote Scottish castle would not do.

True love had no place in their aspirations.

"Pixie, are ye all right?"

"My heart is raw, and I do not look forward to a confrontation with my parents. I hope they are out visiting relatives. I'd like the chance to talk to Holly and Dahlia alone first. Dahlia will be curious about the flowers, of course."

Indeed, what a sight it was to see hundreds of flowers, all with a romantic significance, piled in the Duke of Stoke's home. Red carnations, tulips, and roses. Purple lilacs.

But fortune did not smile on her. Both of her parents were seated in the parlor with her sisters and looked up with disapproving expressions when she and Robbie walked in.

"Oh, dear." Holly set down her teacup and rose to give her a hug.

Heather nodded. "It has all fallen apart."

"What happened?" Her father set aside his cake, his brow furrowed in worry as he also rose. "Is Tilbury attempting to back out of the wedding?"

"No. Quite the opposite. He won't release me from our betrothal."

Her mother inhaled sharply. "Why ever would he do such a thing? And why would you want him to?" She glared at Robbie. "Captain MacLauren, I see you've had a hand in this. I'll ask you to leave now and cause no more trouble for my daughter."

Heather put a hand on Robbie's arm to keep him exactly where he belonged…by her side. "Trouble? He's been trying to unravel the trouble I've caused. I do not love Tilbury, and he does not love me. If you must know, he is madly in love with the Duke of Stoke's daughter, Lady Melinda."

Her mother did not appear moved in the least. "So what? You have him, and she does not."

She made a choked sound and shook her head in disbelief. "That is entirely the point. I cannot marry someone who does not love me. Would you wish this on me? Having to spend the rest of my life knowing my husband is dreaming of someone else, pining for another, and thinking of this other woman whenever he looks at me? I am trying to be rid of him. He is being most uncooperative about it."

Her father resumed his seat beside her mother. "Then the wedding will take place?"

Heather cast him a stubborn look. "No, I'm going to stop it."

"Out of the question." Her father stormed to his feet. "Do you realize the consequences to us?"

Her mother's teacup rattled as she set it down hastily, almost spilling its contents over the lip. "You are not stopping it, Heather. Do be serious. Have you packed yet? Is your wedding gown carefully stored and ready for tomorrow? You'll have to do something with your hair.

You cannot put it up in so simple a fashion. It must be something elegant, something fitting for a marchioness."

"I shall wear my hair in braids and attend in my bedroom slippers." She tucked herself closer to Robbie. "I will show up tomorrow, but only in the hope Lord Tilbury will halt the ceremony. If he does not, I will have no choice but to run off to Scotland. I cannot marry him. Robbie...that is, Captain MacLauren and I have discussed it. We understand there may be repercussions. We will do whatever necessary to protect you."

Her father glowered at Robbie. "You're to blame for this, putting wild ideas into my daughter's head. I've heard about you. I know the sort of man you are."

"The best sort," Heather interjected. "Joshua and Ronan would not be friends with him otherwise. Lord Liverpool wouldn't value his opinions, nor would the Scottish lords trust him to serve as their parliamentary liaison if he weren't of the finest character."

"Daughter, you do not know what he's really like," her mother said. "At least Tilbury makes no pretense about his feelings. But Captain MacLauren will break your heart as he has done with countless other women."

"It isn't true...well, it may have been at one time. But no longer." She turned to Robbie for help.

He took her hand. "Heather knows my past. I've made no secret of it. She has my heart and always will. If she accepts to be my wife, I will never give her cause to doubt me."

Her father snorted in disbelief.

She was hurt by her parents' refusal to consider her wishes.

"Papa, we can discuss this later." Dahlia had been listening to the exchanges and now spoke up. "Robbie, then our ploy with the flowers failed? Tell me what happened."

Her father frowned. "Dahlia, you were involved in this?"

She nodded. "Holly and I are now married to men who love us.

We want the same for Heather. So, yes. I helped. And I shall continue to help in any way I can."

"Me, too." Holly tipped her chin up, casting her parents the most defiant look Heather had ever seen on her sister. Holly's temperament was such that she would suffer in silence and eat her insides out before ever forcing a confrontation.

Heather smiled at her, liking Joshua's influence on her. She was ready to stand up to their parents, no more appeasing their desires.

Her father threw his hands up in evident frustration. "Heather, if I could lock you in your bedchamber, I would. Mark my words, you will never be happy with Captain MacLauren. I don't know what he's promised you or whether he's even made you any promises. Not that it matters. Rogues like him never keep to their word."

The remark only made her trust Robbie more. Not only would he keep every promise, he'd pledge his life to hold true to it.

Her mother sniffed. "Indeed, what can he ever offer you? A fine carriage? An elegant home? On his wages? You'll be living in a tent and riding on a caisson. He's a mere captain."

"As are Dahlia's husband and mine," Holly pointed out.

"It is entirely different," her mother retorted. "The Braydens are wealthy and established in London. Set aside your romantic notions and think logically for once, Heather. I will grant you Captain MacLauren is a very handsome man, but what else does he have in his favor? And do not toss out that he is a close relation to the Earl of Caithness. I know very well who he is and how low his chances are of ever inheriting anything from that old man."

Heather was appalled. "Robbie, I'm so sorry. Please accept my apologies. You know I do not feel this way."

"Aye, lass. I know. I dinna take offense. They only want what they believe is best for ye." He covered her hand with his own. "Ye're with yer family now. I have other matters to attend to. Send word to the Caithness townhouse if ye have need of me."

She sensed he wanted to kiss her, for his eyes were tender and gleaming, but he merely gave her hand a light squeeze. "I'll see ye tomorrow."

He nodded to the others and strode out.

Heather watched him leave and did not turn back to her parents until she heard the front door close behind him.

Her shoulders sagged the moment he left the house.

She took the seat beside Holly's and sighed.

Holly gave her hand a light squeeze. "It will work out. Don't give up hope. It must work out. *The Book of Love* won't let you down."

Heather shook her head. "It isn't magical. I suppose it had to fail sometime."

"Well, I'm not giving up on it. It worked for Joshua and me, and I was no easy match to make."

She smiled.

At least Holly had found her happiness.

So had Dahlia.

"Thank you for all your help, Dahlia. It was a good plan, but I interfered with it, and it went awry. Lady Withnall took me to the Duke of Stoke's home and gave me the chance to speak to him and Lady Melinda. I should have excused myself and left immediately afterward. But I stayed, not that I had much choice. Lady Melinda had no intention of letting me go, and Lady Withnall seemed to be in agreement with her. I think the duke just wanted to throttle me."

"Oh, dear." Her mother put a hand to her throat. "I hope you haven't made an enemy of him."

Heather rolled her eyes. "He had better hold his tongue, or he'll make an enemy of *me*. But no, he's a smart man and loves his daughter. He will do whatever he can to see Melinda happy, and in this matter, he knows I will do all I can to help him."

Dahlia cast her a grim look. "Assuming there is anything possible to be done in these final hours. They are a pair, Melinda and Tilbury.

They're so caught up in their own schemes, they can't see how much they are hurting each other and everyone around them."

Her father rose and turned to face them all. "Schemes or not, our lives will be ruined if you do not go through with the wedding. Have you no consideration for your mother or for myself? He shall destroy us socially, financially, and in every other way possible. We shall be pariahs in York."

Heather had worried about precisely this. It was the only hold Tilbury had on her. "Captain MacLauren's family would always welcome you."

Her father was unmoved. In truth, he was turning apoplectic. "And what are we to do up in Caithness? Toss cabers and listen to the whine of those annoying bagpipes? No, Heather. You do not have our consent to break it off with the marquess. You will show up tomorrow morning at St. Mary's and exchange wedding vows with that man."

Her sisters looked stricken, but she held them off when they sought to defend her. "I appreciate the effort. It's all right. I understand what I must do."

Her father sank back in his seat beside her mother. "That's right. You just remember your duty to your mother and me."

Her mother glanced up as though suddenly struck by a thought. "We've never met your marquess. Holly, I think you must invite him over to meet us tonight."

She, Holly, and Dahlia stared at each other, stunned.

Heather did not know whether to laugh or cry. How could they consider such a thing after all she'd told them? Well, crying was out of the question because she'd already shed too many tears. So, she laughed.

Then her sisters began to laugh.

Joshua and Ronan walked in to find them holding their sides, tears of mirth streaming down their cheeks.

"Love, are you all right?" Joshua asked Holly.

She nodded and told them the reason, as well as all else that had happened.

"Oh, hell." Ronan groaned and went to the sideboard to pour himself a stiff drink. "Where's Robbie?"

"I kicked him out," her father said with uncalled for smug satisfaction because they all knew Robbie would not have left unless it suited his purpose to go.

Joshua understood this and turned to Heather. "Where is he now?"

"He said he was returning to his townhouse." She thought on it a moment. "Well, what he said precisely was to send word to him at the Caithness townhouse if I had need of him."

Ronan nodded. "Do you think he's there now?"

Heather shook her head. "No, he hasn't given up on changing Tilbury's mind. But I sense he's through with negotiation."

She cast a wincing glance at her parents before returning her gaze to her two brothers-in-law. "As I said, no more negotiation. He's primed for open warfare."

Her mother gasped. "Warfare? And you've encouraged this? What will he do to the marquess?"

CHAPTER SIXTEEN

Heather glanced up at the sky the following morning as she descended Uncle John's carriage to enter St. Mary's Church. The sky was a glorious deep blue that jumped out and smacked you in the face with its brightness and clarity. Such skies only occurred in late spring or early autumn before the haze of heat or bleakness of winter set in.

"Are you ready, Heather?" Aunt Sophie asked, giving her hand a light pat.

"Yes." It did not seem fair this ignominious day should be so bright and clear, or the breeze so light and gently warming on her skin.

Well, if she decided to make a run to Scotland with Robbie, it couldn't hurt to be running in good weather.

"You look beautiful, my dear," Uncle John said, kissing her cheek.

She had on the pale blue silk gown, the one that was the color of a robin's egg. Her hair was done up in a simple but elegant braided twist with a few wispy curls to frame her face. Rather than don a hat or veil, she'd merely had a few meadow flowers threaded through her hair.

Guests were now arriving, friends and family of hers and of Tilbury's.

By the curious looks everyone cast her as they descended their carriages and stepped inside the church, she knew what they were all thinking. Will she or won't she marry the marquess?

Perhaps some were silently posing the opposite question. Will he or won't he marry the unworthy commoner?

A few did not care a whit what happened and silently posed a third question. Will there or will there not be a wedding breakfast even if there is no wedding? After all, people had to eat—no sense letting all that sumptuous food go to waste.

She scanned the crowd for a sign of Robbie but did not see him.

Her parents arrived.

So did her sisters and their husbands.

So did her cousins and their husbands.

Good. Lots of dukes and earls on her side of the aisle.

Her Uncle George and his wife were present. Also good; they'd require his medical attention if a brawl broke out.

"Heather, we ought to go in," her father said, taking her arm to lead her inside.

She resisted. "Tilbury has not yet arrived. I haven't seen his mother or his sister, either."

She dared not mention Robbie for fear of sending her father into another fit.

Oh, he would be apoplectic soon enough.

She'd taken *The Book of Love* to bed with her last night, reading it thoroughly, especially the chapter on connections and expectations. She'd even made lists regarding Tilbury. Another regarding Robbie. Another she titled "Living in Scotland" and one she'd titled "Living in England." A third, she'd titled "Living in London." A fourth she'd titled "Ruining My Parents," not that there were any advantages to such an outcome, but it helped to think through all the consequences should Tilbury turn out to be a vindictive ogre.

She'd made so many lists into the night, she had run out of writing paper. But by then, she'd given herself enough to work on. More importantly, for the first time, she had read the book with an open heart. She now understood what it meant to listen to what her senses were telling her, instead of denying or forcing the meanings, manipulating them into something else.

The realization of what she needed, what was essential, and could not be compromised, opened her eyes to all she had been missing. Robbie had been trying to teach her this all along. No wonder it tore his heart when she wouldn't listen.

"Where is he?" her mother whispered, trying not to be obvious as she began to fret. "Has that despicable Captain MacLauren harmed him, do you think?"

"No, and he isn't despicable. He's honorable. Too honorable to harm anyone. He isn't a brute."

Her father scoffed.

She held her tongue, for they would soon have the hot air knocked out of them. Tilbury was now half an hour late to his wedding. Also, he had not bothered to send over a bride token the night before for her to wear with her wedding gown this morning. No heirloom necklace or ring. No brooch bearing the family crest or encrusted with precious gems.

While her parents were getting worked up over this neglect, she was gladdened by it. Was this Tilbury's way of telling her she was released from their betrothal? Perhaps he was too overset by the events of yesterday to think of anything else and was now passed out drunk in his study?

The church doors suddenly flew open, and Lady Withnall sauntered in.

Thuck, thuck, thuck.

Her cane tapped against the marble floor as she walked up front and took a seat between her friend, Lady Eloise Dayne, and Heather's parents. All whispering had stopped. To Heather, it seemed no one dared breathe as the little harridan had passed each pew and cast her beady-eyed gaze on those gathered.

But once she sat, the guests began to sigh in relief and grow restless.

Bishop Farraday cleared his phlegmy throat. He had been associated with the Tilbury family for decades and had always been the one to officiate at births, deaths, marriages, and other such rites. Heather thought perhaps he had been officiating for centuries, for he appeared doddering and creaky.

Tilbury was now forty-five minutes late.

Bishop Farraday was still *cheching* beside her, making that horrible noise one made when clearing clumps from one's throat. He then snuffled it back up his nose. "Someone ought to ride over to his lordship's residence."

"No need," Lady Withnall intoned but gave no further explanation. She merely turned to Aunt Sophie and complimented her on her lovely gown.

"Thank you, Lady Withnall," Sophie replied with a wry smile.

"Let's give it a few more minutes," Joshua suggested. "I'll ride over if he does not appear within the hour." He turned to Heather and arched an eyebrow as though silently asking her what was going on?

She shook her head, being as much in the dark as he.

The guests began to rise from their seats and mill about. Many were now whispering, a few chortling, and there was a persistent buzz echoing off the gracefully arched ceiling.

An hour had passed.

"I'll go with you, Josh," Ronan said, drawing out his fob and marking the time, although it wasn't necessary since the church bells now rang to mark the passage of the hour. *Sext.* The noon hour. The mealtime hour for many.

There would be a lot of privileged stomachs rumbling about now.

Heather glanced at her sisters and tried not to smile. She was never more eager to be thought of as a laughingstock. Was it possible? Had Tilbury been struck by lightning? Or rather, hit by sudden clarity? Was he going to jilt her?

Please, please. Let it be so.

Joshua and Ronan had taken no more than a step when there was another commotion by the front doors, and Tilbury strode in.

Heather's heart sank.

Then she noticed Robbie marching in behind him.

Both men were dressed quite elegantly and were remarkably well-groomed. It was to be expected of Tilbury, for he always dressed with immaculate care, and every garment he owned was the finest Savile Row had to offer.

One would think he would do no less for his wedding day, even if neither the bride nor groom wished to be married to each other.

As for Robbie, he always looked spectacular even when drunk and falling off walls. But he wore his dress uniform and had clearly taken care to look his best for the occasion. Her heart began to flip-flop. It was unavoidable, couldn't be helped.

She loved Robbie.

Bishop Farraday immediately asked the question on everyone's mind. "My lord, is there to be a wedding?"

"That depends entirely on Miss Farthingale." His gaze swept across the gathering of family and friends before coming to rest on her. "Do you wish to be married?"

She tried to read his expression, but she was quite awful at understanding men anyway and could discern nothing by it. "Yes, I do, Lord Tilbury." She heard gasps of relief—her parents, no doubt—amid the gasps of surprise. From his side of the aisle, she heard gasps of disappointment. "Yes, I do wish to be married." She tipped her head up to look him steadily in the eyes. "But not to you."

Perhaps she ought to have phrased it more politely or begged for a private word. Too late now. The flying buttresses upon the arched ceiling once more resounded with excited whispers. Indeed, the church fairly hummed as those whispers circulated about the vast chamber.

Her parents were on their feet, attempting to reach her and draw her aside. Her sisters held them back.

Heather turned to Robbie, her bones melting as he returned her smile with an affectionate grin of his own. "I wish to be married to Captain MacLauren, if he'll have me."

Tilbury did not appear to mind at all. "Will you have her, Captain MacLauren?"

"Aye, my lord." He kept his gaze on Heather. "I love the lass."

"Well, that greatly eases my mind," Tilbury said, smiling at her with more warmth than she'd ever seen out of him in all the months of their betrothal. "You see, I cannot marry you, Miss Farthingale."

"And why not?" her father shouted.

"Because I am already married." His grin broadened so that it stretched from ear to ear. There was a lightness in his eyes she'd never seen before. He waited for the din of the crowd to die down before explaining. "Lady Melinda and I were married early this morning. She is now Lady Tilbury. Captain MacLauren stood beside me as my witness."

Heather let out a whoop and tossed her bouquet of flowers into the air. She threw herself into Tilbury's arms as he held them out to her, and he spun her in his arms, the two of them laughing and more joyful than ever at the prospect of *not* marrying each other.

Bishop Farraday looked befuddled.

Lady Withnall had caught her bouquet. *Oh, heavens!* The lore had it that whomsoever caught a bride's bouquet would be next to marry. No. It wasn't possible. There was not a man alive who would wish to marry her. Was there?

"Don't be ridiculous," Lady Withnall grumbled, reading Heather's thoughts. "It only works if you throw the flowers *after* you are married, not before." She tossed them back to Heather. "Stop gawking at me. Go marry your handsome Scot. Be quick about it. I have winnings to collect from the Strand bookmakers."

"Gladly, but how is it possible? We would need a special license and my father's permission. How—"

Robbie withdrew a parchment from his breast pocket. "A special license like this one?" He turned to her father. "Will ye shame yer daughter and deny her heart's desire? I'll be marrying her with or without yer permission. We only need to ride to Scotland to make it happen. But yer daughter deserves better, and it would break her heart not to have yer blessing. So, I ask ye, please. Put her sweet, soft heart at ease."

Her parents looked exceedingly pained, but after a long moment, her father nodded. "All we ever wanted was happiness for our daughters. Yes, you have our blessing."

Heather did not believe such joy was possible.

As the men retired to the church rector's office to quickly sign the necessary papers, Heather spent the minutes hugging members of her family. When she heard the men returning, she made her way to Lady Withnall and fiercely hugged her. "I had nothing to do with it," the old woman grumbled. "It was all your handsome Scot's doing."

Heather laughed. "Then I shall hug him, too."

And she did before they exchanged their wedding vows and immediately afterward as well. "We're married, Robbie," she whispered, holding on to him with all her being, and was surprised by the depth of feeling he expressed in response.

"*Mo chridhe*," he whispered back, holding her in his arms and returning her hug with an exquisitely tender kiss. "I love ye, Mrs. MacLauren."

As everyone hopped back in their carriages and made their way to Tilbury's residence for the much-awaited wedding breakfast, Heather noticed Robbie had stepped away and was bent on one knee before the statue of a saint in a quiet corner of the church. She went to his side but did not speak so as not to disturb him.

He sensed her presence and took her hand.

"Married five minutes, and you're already praying for a way out?"

she teased, sinking beside him.

"Och, my pixie. Ye know it is no' so. I loved ye at first sight. When ye agreed to marry the marquess, I despaired of losing ye. My heart was in pieces. I could no' bear to stay in London and watch the two of ye together. But it dinna matter how far away I rode…and Caithness is at the end of the world. I could no' get ye out of my shattered heart."

"Robbie, I was so stupid. I'm so sorry I put you through such torment."

"It does no' matter now. There's no blame to be cast. Ye're my wife. I'll love ye forever. My heart is healed. I was just giving thanks to Saint Brigid for the miracle she brought about. I got used to praying to her on the battlefield. But I dinna always behave myself, and I'm sure she felt the need to kick my arse a little, or she would have brought Tilbury and Melinda to their senses much sooner."

She kissed him lightly on the lips. "I needed a few swift kicks myself, didn't I?"

"No, sweetheart. Ye were trying to follow a dream." He lifted her up along with him. "Do ye love me, my pixie?"

"Hopelessly, utterly, and desperately. Will you tell me how Saint Brigid brought this miracle about? Were you giving her thanks for delivering *The Book of Love* to you?"

"Well, in this instance, we needed all the miracles and magic available to us. Tilbury was a hard nut to crack. So was Lady Melinda."

Heather nodded thoughtfully. "I don't think it was a miracle or a magical book so much as your tenacity and refusal to ever give up hope."

"I'm a stubborn Scot, that's all."

"I'm glad for it. I doubt anyone else would have put up with my stubborn determination. I spent last night searching my heart. I knew as I came here and stood waiting for Tilbury, that I could never accept to be his wife. I was ready to crawl on my knees in front of all our guests and beg him not to hurt my parents. Even if my pleas fell upon deaf ears and he took everything they owned, Holly, Dahlia, and I would always look after them. They would never be destitute because we love them and would always protect them and provide for them."

She groaned and cast him a wistful smile. "They were not very kind to you, but they are not bad people. They only meant for their daughters to have the best, as misguided as their intentions were. They will come around and love you as I do."

"I know, my pixie. Even if they never warm to me, it does no' matter. They are yer parents, and ye love them. Fortunately, they will no' have to worry about reprisals from Tilbury now. He is the one who broke off the betrothal."

"You won't find a bride happier to be jilted at the altar." She could not suppress her happiness. "How in heaven's name did you convince Lady Melinda to marry him?"

CHAPTER SEVENTEEN

ROBBIE WAITED UNTIL the wedding breakfast was over and all the guests returned to their homes before he began his explanation. The breakfast had taken place at Lord Tilbury's home, but the marquess had not remained with them. He'd gone off with a flourish, leaving everyone to the feast that had already been prepared.

Certainly, this wedding day would be spoken of long afterward.

"Enjoy," he had told Robbie, taking him aside before he'd left and pointed to the resplendent array of game fowl, roasted meats, loins of pork, and for lighter fare, puddings, cheese, fruit, bread, and cakes of every variety imaginable set out on tables in his opulent ballroom. "This is my gift to you and Heather for putting you through such torment. You have my sincere apologies."

The doors had been thrown open, and smaller tables and chairs could be seen around the shade trees in his manicured garden. More tables and chairs were placed indoors for those who did not wish to be out in the sun. The marquess left as soon as the festivities were underway, heading to the Duke of Stoke's residence to take his new bride on the wedding trip, originally planned for him and Heather.

Robbie had glanced around once left alone with Heather, noting the abundance and splendor. "Love, I canno' offer ye the grand tour he–"

"You offered me your heart, Robbie. Nothing can be better. Who cares where we are as long as we're together?" She had followed his gaze around the ballroom and then smiled at him. "Beautiful, isn't it? So is his home. Magnificent paintings, delicate vases, splendidly woven carpets. But these are just things. They are no replacement for the joy I feel when I am beside you. They are no replacement for love."

And that put an end to any doubts he might have felt about depriving Heather of the riches a marquess could offer.

"Tell us, Robbie. We are itching to know how you pulled this off," Dahlia said.

It was now evening, and they were seated in the parlor of the Caithness townhouse, joined by Heather's sisters and their husbands. Her parents had gone off with the family elders. Robbie silently reminded himself to thank John, Rupert, and George for keeping her parents occupied. While they were resigned to her daughter marrying him, they had not yet accepted him with open arms. He did not want their frowns or snide comments to dampen Heather's spirits, for unlike their daughter, they were quite impressed by all the beautiful objects in Tilbury's home and regretted their daughter not having them.

"Yes, we are all busting to know," Holly agreed. "How did you manage to bring this about?"

Robbie took Heather's hand as he sat beside her on the settee. "I knew we'd won yesterday the moment Lady Melinda slipped the sapphire ring on her finger."

They had returned to the Earl of Caithness's residence quite full from the wedding celebration. But the Crawfords had insisted on setting out more refreshments for them. They now fussed over Heather as they did so and interrupted his explanation. "It is pleased we are ye had the good sense to marry our Robbie," Mr. Crawford took it upon himself to tell her.

Heather laughed and responded with sincere warmth, not a trace of snobbery in the soft lilt of her voice. "Thank you, Mr. Crawford. It took some doing, but true love won out. Didn't it?"

Mrs. Crawford became teary-eyed. "Och, we knew it from the very first time he set eyes on ye. This is what he told us. I've met the lass I'm going to marry."

Robbie dismissed them with a groan. "Dinna give away all my secrets."

Fortunately, his friends were not going to give him a hard time since they'd felt no different about their wives. He'd never met two men who were more doting, besotted fools than Joshua and Ronan. "Ye wish to hear the rest of the story?"

"Yes," Heather said, squeezing his hand, and the others nodded.

"As I said, she put on the ring. He'd made an arse of himself, shocked everyone by openly courting Melinda the day before his wedding day, standing amid a roomful of flowers, prepared to make a laughingstock of himself before all their friends. I was afraid his heart would rupture when he saw Heather seated beside Melinda. But ye'd done yer job, lass."

"I thought you didn't want me to be there?"

"I dinna, but someone needed to talk to Melinda, and ye were right to do it. She had to be assured her marquess dinna love ye and that ye dinna love him. Her father also had to be made to understand just how deeply his daughter and Tilbury cared for each other."

"And how badly they'd botched their own courtship," Ronan added.

"Aye." He grinned at Heather. "I thought I'd made a mess of ours. In truth, I never courted ye properly, and for this, I am deeply sorry."

Joshua laughed. "Don't feel too badly. I'm sure you would have botched it with or without Tilbury's interference."

Robbie chuckled. "Thank ye, Josh. Glad ye always have my back."

"But Tilbury takes the prize without question," Ronan said. "He did everything wrong when it came to winning Melinda's heart."

"Och, aye. All he ever had to do was trust her and be honest with her, let her know how important she was to him."

Dahlia sighed. "By making a fool of himself, she finally got the message. I'm glad I could be of help."

"An immense help, Dahlia. It took everything to move that pair. The flowers were perfect. She understood their meaning, and it finally softened her heart. Then the ring. She realized what the sapphires represented. Tilbury finally did something right by telling her what the diamonds meant to him."

He raked a hand through his hair and continued. "As I mentioned, Heather was right to visit Stoke and his daughter. But I will admit, my heart stopped when I saw her seated beside Melinda. I canno' imagine what went through Tilbury's mind as he walked in and saw them together. But the shock of it might have helped to finally knock down his barriers and allow him to stand in front of all their guests with his heart exposed. He left it right there in the center of the floor for her to stomp on if she pleased, dinna he?"

"I never believed he could leave himself so open and vulnerable," Heather remarked.

"Nor did I, lass. That is what worried me most. But he finally managed to express what he'd hidden inside all the while, and this is what it took to convince Melinda. As I said, when she put on the ring, I knew we'd won. All I had to do afterward was find Tilbury before he ran off and did something stupid. Although I dinna think he'd go very far because he is a man driven by duty, and he meant to show up at St. Mary's for his wedding today."

"Where was he when you tracked him down?"

"Drinking heavily in his study. I told him to stop drinking and stay put because he'd won. He dinna believe me at first, but he finally relented and gave me his word. Then I went to Stoke and Melinda and dragged them over to Tilbury's home. Some of their guests were still there, but I dinna care. Melinda was still wearing his ring, and I needed to get them together before she took it off."

Ronan arched an eyebrow. "You dragged them?"

"Lifted is more like it." Robbie grimaced. "I picked her up and flung her over my shoulder. The lass is stubborn and too proud for her own good. But her father understood what needed to be done. He dinna let his footmen stop me. The three of us rode over to Tilbury's together, and then we left her and Tilbury alone in his study to sort it out."

Holly laughed. "That was brave of you. How did you know they weren't going to kill each other?"

"Before I left to fetch her, I told him what to do."

"And that was?" Dahlia asked.

"To shut up and kiss her. The less talking he did, the better. The advice applied to both of them. They dinna know how to speak to each other without wounding with their words."

Joshua glanced at Holly and cast her an affectionate smile. "Good thing kisses work, or we'd all be in trouble. Men never think clearly when we're in love. If we open our mouths, we're going to say something stupid. The less said, the better. But how did you manage the special license? His license had to have named Heather."

Robbie nodded. "That's where Stoke's influence came to the rescue. He took us straight to the archbishop of London. Stoke tore up the first special license and stood over the archbishop while he issued a new one for Tilbury and Melinda. But as a favor to Dahlia, the duke had the archbishop issue a special license for Heather and me."

Ronan arched an eyebrow. "He did this for Dahlia? My love, should I be worried?"

She laughed and patted his hand. "I think you are safe...for the moment. There are so few people who will tell him the truth. He finds me delightful and refreshing. I'm sure he will soon find me irritating and opinionated."

She then turned to Robbie. "I like that he thought of you and Heather. He is a decent man but so lost without his wife. Theirs was a love match, although I'm sure it began as a business alliance among families. Having known love, he wanted this for his daughter. He must have appreciated the effort it took for you to bring it about."

"Aye, he did." He smiled as he spoke, now that all he'd accomplished in the span of a day was sinking in. "I also suggested the archbishop marry them on the spot. Stoke heartily agreed. He loves his daughter, but she's a stubborn handful. And Tilbury can be a dolt, too. The sooner they were bound in a holy union, the better for all of us."

"Amen to that," Joshua said.

"When we left the archbishop, Melinda and her father returned to their residence so she could pack for their grand tour."

"The one meant for me," Heather murmured, but she was grinning and looked relieved rather than wistful, so she put Robbie's mind at ease.

"Tilbury returned to his residence with the promise to come to St. Mary's with me and stand by me as Heather and I were married. I thought it would help stem the malicious gossip that might spread about his jilting Heather. She'd be the one hurt, the innocent victim. Is it no' often the case?"

The others agreed.

"We all got our happy ending, although I dinna know how long that pair will be happy if they dinna learn how to talk to each other."

Heather nodded. "This was our perfect ending, just like in *A Midsummer Night's Dream*, the couples awaking and finally properly matched. Robbie, I think you are now Tilbury's best friend. He will turn to you for advice if ever they stumble. I hope Melinda will turn to Dahlia for advice instead of running away from the poor marquess. They could do with *The Book of Love*, but I dare not give it to them. It needs to stay within the family for now."

"Who gets it next?" Joshua asked, genuinely curious.

Heather glanced at her sisters. "We talked it over earlier this afternoon. Our Devonshire cousins will have it next. Juniper, first. We call her June. She's the eldest, about Holly's age. Her sisters, Willow and Camellia, are close in age to me and Dahlia. They'll be coming to London for their debuts. Uncle John just got a letter from his cousin regarding their expected arrival. But it won't be for a few months yet, so we are sending the book to them and urging them to read it before they reach London."

Joshua and Ronan burst out laughing.

"I pity this year's crop of bachelors," Ronan said, grinning at Dahlia."

Joshua agreed. "Fortunately, there are no more Brayden men here for them to wreak havoc on their lives."

"Or MacLauren men," Robbie said, laughing with them.

When their laughter died, Holly rose and took Joshua by the hand. "My love, I think it's time we left these two alone."

Dahlia also rose and locked her arm in Ronan's. "We don't want to disturb Romulus and Violet this evening, but we'll pack up Heather's clothes first thing in the morning and send them over to you." She grinned at Heather. "I think you'll manage just fine tonight in Robbie's care."

They all left in haste.

Robbie found himself on his own with Heather, who was blushing furiously. He took her in his arms, knowing he would have to slowly ease her into the consummation of their marriage.

Warmth washed through his body as he wrapped her in his embrace. They were now husband and wife. It felt so good to know he had the right to claim her for his own without worry of shaming her. "I canno' believe ye're finally mine. I have to pinch myself to make sure this is no dream."

"I know. Robbie, you must be exhausted. Did you get any sleep last night?"

"Not much, my pixie. But it was worth the effort to know I'd have ye in my arms for always."

Her blush deepened. "Shall we go up to bed?"

He cast her a wicked smile. "Aye, lass. That's an excellent idea."

"Do you think I might borrow some of your bedclothes for this evening?"

"No, lass. Ye canno'." He laughed softly. "I dinna have any."

"You don't? What do you wear to bed?"

"I sleep naked as the day I was born." His smile broadened. "I dinna think ye'll need to worry about bedclothes tonight. If ye grow cold, I'll be warming yer sweet body."

She coughed. "Oh, I see."

He led her upstairs to his quarters. The chamber was not very large or opulent. Nevertheless, it was a cozy, inviting room and beautifully appointed. The bed was comfortable and big enough to easily fit both of them.

He was pleased Mrs. Crawford had thought to set out a scented soap, some tooth powder, a hairbrush, and other amenities for Heather. Mr. Crawford had a fire blazing in the hearth, not that they really needed it. But they'd both be undressed soon, so he supposed it was helpful.

The couple had also stocked the room for them, setting out more of the light repast they'd had downstairs. Some ham, fruit, bread, and scones to go with a pot of tea.

While Heather took care of washing up before bed, Robbie removed his boots and jacket, then hastily washed up himself.

When she was done, he took her back in his arms and gave her cheek a light caress. "Let me take the pins from yer hair. Feels good not to worry about where they might drop."

She smiled one of her entrancing pixie smiles and looked up at him with big eyes filled with love. "My heart is racing, Robbie."

"So is mine, lass."

She regarded him dubiously. "But you've done this before."

"Not with anyone I've ever loved. Ye have my heart, I hope ye know this."

She nodded. "I'm glad. I hope you love me deeply and irrevocably because if our wedding night is as calamitous as our courtship, we'll be in trouble."

He laughed and kissed her on the lips, tasting the mint on them from her tooth powder. He liked that her mouth was soft and giving. "I dinna think we'll have a problem, lass," he whispered against her ear and began to feather kisses down her neck, liking when she gasped in response and tilted her neck to give him a better angle.

He soon had her gown unlaced and the pins out of her hair. He buried his hands in the lush cascade of hair, loving the silky feel of it as the long strands slipped through his fingers. "Ye're beautiful, my pixie."

"So are you, Captain MacLauren. There's a wicked glimmer in your eyes."

"A gleam of desire from wanting ye so badly. Lass, yer body has me in a low brain frenzy."

She smiled. "I'm enjoying the sight of your body, too. Would you mind if I touched you?"

"No, I dinna mind. I'm yers now. Do whatever ye please."

She tried to slip the shirt off him but needed his help. Once it was off, he stood motionless as she splayed her small hands across his chest and then ran them up and down his arms. "Your skin is warm."

"That's a polite way of putting it. I'm mad, hot for ye. But I will no' rush ye. We have all night." He slid the gown off her so that it lightly *whooshed* as it fell to the floor.

He admired the roundness of her backside as she bent to retrieve her gown and place it neatly over a chair.

When she returned to his side, he made quick work of her undergarments, taking care to set them over the chair since she had no other clothes here yet and she'd be embarrassed to have to wear something crumpled.

Also, she had yet to experience the heat of passion. Perhaps next time, they would be tearing off their clothes in frantic haste to couple.

The breath caught in his throat as he removed the last of her garments, and she stood naked before him, her body exquisite as she was illuminated by the fire's light.

She looked magical.

Ethereal.

He lifted her in his arms and carried her to bed, settling her in the center of it before turning away a moment to remove his trousers. Her eyes widened when he turned to face her, for he was aroused, and there was no possibility of hiding it. "Did yer sisters explain any—"

"Yes!" She nodded. "They warned me."

"Warned ye?" He gave a groaning laugh. "Dinna fret, lass. Ye'll enjoy our coupling."

She blushed. "They told me this, too."

They spoke no more as he climbed in beside her and shifted her under him. Her body felt creamy and soft beneath him. He slowly began to kiss and touch her, lightly at first, touching his lips to hers and stroking his hand in a gentle caress along her waist and hips.

When he felt her warming to him, he moved his hand upward to cup her breast and run his thumb in a teasing swirl around its tautening bud. At the same time, he began to kiss her along her neck and down to the swell of her breast, finally closing his mouth over it.

She gasped when he gave it a soft lick and began to suckle her rosy bud between his lips.

"Robbie," she whispered urgently, drawing him closer and sweetly clinging to his shoulders.

He loved the lavender scent of her skin. She was a flower, blossoming in the sun, emitting her attractive scent as she warmed to his touch.

Then she was hot to his touch, and all became a dizzying blur as he stroked her and suckled her breasts, and readied her for the intimacy to come. He knew the moment she was ready by the slick heat between her thighs and her soft breaths that now came faster. "Open for me, my love."

He touched his fingers to the nub of her sweet essence to prepare her for their coupling. "Pixie, I love ye," he whispered, entering her and claiming her faithfully and truly as his wife.

CHAPTER EIGHTEEN

H EATHER'S HEART WAS racing as Robbie settled his magnificently muscled body over her slight and slender one. He was now pressed against her, big and broad-shouldered, exuding power and strength. She ran her hands along his arms that were hard and sinewed like those of a trained warrior. His stomach was flat, and his legs were long and lean. "Trust me, lass?"

"I do, Robbie." Her body thrummed in anticipation of what would come next. He was aroused, she could tell by his quickening breaths and the heat of his skin against hers.

She wasn't certain how the size of him would fit inside her. But her sisters had told her it would, speaking with shocking frankness, and this now helped to calm her as *the moment* approached.

He propped his elbows on either side of her so as not to crush her, but she found herself enjoying the weight of him atop her and felt somehow comforted by it. The touch of his roughened hands as he caressed her skin made her tingle everywhere.

Then he began the timeless mating ritual, cautiously at first, so that he would not hurt her. She closed her eyes to absorb all these new sensations, the intimate strokes of his hand. The warmth of his mouth upon her skin. The heat of his tongue upon her breasts.

"Ye taste so sweet, my pixie," he whispered, somehow managing to retain control while she was slipping into sensations she'd never experienced before. She responded to him with a hot, pulsing need, her blood now fiery, and her body ready to take him in to fill her emptiness with the strength of him.

She felt only the slightest discomfort when he first entered her, but once she was used to him, all she felt was heat and an exquisitely building pressure as he embedded himself inside of her and claimed her for his own.

But she felt so much more with his every thrust, for their bodies spoke to each other. Their language was passion, and their dance was a timeless waltz of love.

With each movement, each kiss, they were binding their hearts as well as their souls.

She breathed in his musky scent, learned the curves and rippling bulges of his muscled torso, tasted the warmth of his lips so that all of him would be seared into her memory and her soul.

He was doing the same, memorizing her touch and scent, and searing them into his soul so that she would forever be a part of him.

She moved with him, her hips easily guided by his patient and gentle hands toward something powerful and eternal she had never experienced before.

She sighed and softly moaned his name. "Robbie…"

"Aye, my pixie," he whispered and kissed her on the lips.

She felt the slow simmer of heat and longing in her blood and felt it begin to course like fire through her veins. An unexpected pressure built inside of her as he thrust into her. Tense. Relentless. Volcanic. The feeling was so intense, she felt on the verge of erupting. "Robbie."

"Don't hold back, my love."

She couldn't even if she wanted to.

He stroked her limbs and suckled her breasts, knowing the sensitive spots on her body better than she did, knowing just how to touch her and arouse her in fiery torment. She shuddered as his tongue licked across the tips of her breasts.

Oh, that felt so good.

"*Mo chridhe*, ye're so lovely," he whispered, taking her soft cries into his mouth in an incredibly delicious kiss as he continued to move inside of her, gracefully. Powerfully. Molten fire swept through her body, then all she saw was starlight, and her body felt weightless, evaporated in a pleasurable heat as he transported her to the stars.

She clung tightly to his shoulders, loving the hard, sculpted beauty of them. "Oh, Robbie."

"I know, lass." He growled softly and quickly followed with his release. He shuddered, spilling his liquid heat into her as he joined her on the starlit journey.

She could only describe it as wondrous, for this is how it felt to her.

His arms were gentle, and he cradled her in them while they spent themselves, drifting down from their heights together.

She felt languid and satiated.

He looked upon her with so much love, he stole her breath away. "What are you thinking, Robbie?"

"Och, lass. I'm thinking ye're the most beautiful vision I've ever beheld." He began to feather gentle kisses on her face and along her body.

Both their bodies were furnaces, giving off heat.

Her skin was warm and damp. So was his.

His eyes were emerald embers, smoldering and shimmering, his smile wickedly affectionate.

She remained in his embrace, sighing as he lightly stroked her hip and caressed her everywhere. She rested her head against his chest, enjoying the deep rumble of his voice as he spoke again. "I knew ye had to be mine when I first met ye and learned yer name was Heather. It is a fine Scots name."

She laughed softly. "I've never been to Scotland. I don't know why my parents named me that."

"They were guided by destiny. They took one look at yer pixie eyes and yer golden-brown hair and knew ye were meant to be a Highlander's wife. Ye were probably born with the sweet scent of lavender on yer skin."

"I'm sure I did not open my eyes. I doubt I had any hair other than a few stray tufts that resembled dandelion fuzz. And I probably smelled of spittle," she teased.

"No, lass. Ye were the most beautiful babe ever born."

She kissed his chest. "If you say so."

She snuggled against him, breathing in the heat and clean maleness of him. "Was it all right, Robbie?"

He chuckled. "Do ye mean *the deed*? Aye, lass. It was nice. More than nice. Pixie, ye fill my heart with gladness. How do ye feel? Did I hurt ye?"

"Only for the one brief moment. But it quickly passed, and the rest of it was quite splendid. My body is still tingling."

"So's mine."

She rose on one elbow to look at him, loving the naughty arch of his eyebrow and the grin on his handsome face. "Don't tease me. I'm a rank beginner. But I think I shall improve over time."

He cupped her cheek. "Ye were perfect. Soft and warm and responsive. Ye need never worry about disappointing me because ye never will. Ye'll always give me pleasure. We dinna make love with only our bodies, but with our hearts as well. Did ye feel it, my pixie?"

"I did." She nodded.

Robbie was tired from the lack of sleep over the past two days, so she said nothing more and drifted to sleep in his arms. He dozed off before she did, but after a few hours, she awoke and stole a few moments to watch the play of moonlight upon his face.

His was an exquisite face. Fine, firm jaw. Nicely shaped mouth. Eyes that stole one's breath away with a mere glance. They were closed now and yet still felt vibrant.

She touched his cheek lightly, curious as to the sensation of the bristled hairs growing back on his cheeks and jaw. He would shave in the morning, but for now, the stubble was hers to touch and stroke.

His eyes flickered open.

"Robbie, I'm sorry. I didn't mean to wake you."

"I dinna need much rest. How do ye feel?" He shifted so he faced her, his muscles rippling like the smooth ripple of water on the glass surface of a lake.

"I feel happy."

He caressed her cheek. "And yer body?"

She grinned. "Also happy."

He fell back against his pillow with a chuckle and drew her atop him. Her thigh grazed him, and she felt him throb to attention. "Dinna mind me, lass. I will no' take ye like this again tonight. Ye'll be too sore in the morning if I do."

She tried to hide her disappointment. "Oh, I suppose it's for the best then."

"But there are other ways." He shifted their positions so that she found herself under his big body.

"What are you going to do?"

"Make love to ye with my heart." He bent to kiss her own rapidly beating heart, then took the rose tip of her breast into his mouth and swirled his tongue over it. His fingers found their way lower to her most intimate spot.

She responded to him quickly, her body once more molten and erupting in flames. When he shifted lower, replacing his fingers with his tongue, she meant to tell him that his lips seemed to be doing all the work, not his heart.

Then she realized she was wrong.

Everything Robbie did to her and for her, everything he thought and felt, his every protective urge and his every sacrifice, was a consequence of his caring for her and valuing her above his own life.

When she erupted in splendor, and he took her back in his arms, she knew this was all that mattered, their caring and giving to each other.

This is how their marriage would always remain strong.

She rested her cheek against his chest and heard the rhythmic pounding of his heart, so strong and steady. "This is how it shall always beat for ye," he whispered and then kissed her.

She smiled.

Yes, this was perfect.

This was the heart of love.

EPILOGUE

Caithness, Scotland
June 1821

ROBBIE HAD WORRIED Heather would grow despondent the further they rode north and away from London and her family. But he was pleased to see he had fretted needlessly. In truth, she seemed to be happy and excited to meet his family and made not a complaint the entire journey, which was not always an easy one. It had rained hard more than a time or two, and the roads were often rugged, causing their carriage to rock and jounce.

He'd brought Gallant home with him, for the trusted steed never left his side. This slowed down their travel since they could not simply change horses at a coaching inn and ride on. Gallant needed to rest, as well as be groomed and fed. However, he was a sturdy beast, and they did not lose all that much time, or so Robbie liked to believe.

But today, the sky was a deep, bright blue, and the sun was golden. Only a few white clouds sailed overhead, moved along by an unhurried and gentle breeze. Even the hawks seemed to be lazily gliding overhead, too busy enjoying the day to seriously hunt for prey.

The gray stone fortress known as Dornoch Castle had come into view several miles back, large and imposing upon the hillock overlooking the firth flowing out to the North Sea.

"Grandda!" Robbie said with delight as his granduncle gave a whoop and hurried down the steps of the castle to greet him. The older man gave no heed to decorum, grabbing him by the shoulders and hugging him as soon as he had emerged from the carriage.

"Is it true, lad? Ye're married?" He tried to look beyond Robbie to the woman still in the carriage, for he'd given him no time to help Heather climb down. "She must be truly special to have tamed ye. I never saw a lad more broken up when ye were home last winter. But we're in full summer now, and if ye were a rose, ye'd be the brightest bloom in the garden. Look at ye, all puffed up and grinning with pride."

"Och, dinna call me a rose, ye pawky old man." He could not help but smile as he helped Heather down and set her gently on her feet. "Grandda, this is my wife, Heather. She's the lass I was broken up over. Ye can understand why, can ye no'?"

His granduncle's expression turned mawkishly tender. "Aye, laddie."

Robbie groaned. "Bollocks, are ye going to cry?"

"It is an earl's privilege, is it not? What's wrong with shedding a tear or two? I'm so happy for ye both. She's a beauty. And she has a bonnie name, too. But I thought ye said she was a Sassenach."

Heather grinned. "I am. It is a pleasure to meet you, my lord."

His granduncle stopped her before she could curtsey. "We'll have none o' that, lass. Ye're a Caithness now, and I could not be more blessed. Robbie affectionately calls me his *grandda,* and I hope ye will call me that, too. Och, what a blessing! Malcolm has his beautiful Anne. Thad has his Penelope, the only lass he's ever loved or ever will love. And now my Robbie has come home with a heart full of joy because of ye. I only hope Augustus has as good a fortune as my other lads have had. I love them all as though they were my own sons."

"I'm sure he will," Robbie said, turning a moment to Heather. "Augustus is my cousin. Thad's brother. He remained on the Continent in command of an elite unit of Scots Greys. He spent the last five years helping Lord Castlereagh secure the peace. But he's on his way home now. He's always been the most sensible of us all. I'm sure he'll find a solemn, sensible Scottish girl and settle down with her upon his return."

Heather shook her head and laughed. "He's fortunate he'll be up here and not in London when my Devonshire cousins arrive. I'm sure Uncle John and Aunt Sophie are already cringing."

He kissed her lightly on the lips. "Little chance of his encountering them."

He turned her to face the castle. "What do ye think, lass? This is my grandda's home. Malcolm and Anne live here with him. The place is overrun with their children now. But they're sweet little beasties. I know ye'll love them, and they'll love you. Where are they, grandda?"

"In town. They'll be home soon. And this is yer home, too," the old man said in earnest. "Forever, if ye wish it to be."

"I know. But we're only here for a visit. Lord Liverpool wants me to stay on as military liaison." He glanced at Heather. "So, I've agreed to another two years."

Heather nodded. "But I won't let him stay longer in his position if he's only doing it for my sake. If he wants to return to Caithness, then this is where we'll settle."

"That's a good lass ye are, and a fine wife ye'll make my Robbie. Thank ye. My heart would be filled with sorrow if I thought the lad was unhappy. But I see now that he will never be, so long as he has ye by his side."

He turned to Robbie as they walked toward the massive stone structure that towered over the town. One could hear the distant roar of waves pounding the cliffside. Robbie looked forward to showing Heather the magnificent view of the sea from their bedchamber window. They would also have a view of the town and nearby hills that were dotted with wildflowers all summer long, he'd earlier told her.

"Robbie," his granduncle said, leaning in to whisper in his ear.

"Have ye noticed? Yer Heather looks like a little pixie, does she no'?"

"Och, grandda, I had not noticed." He smiled and winked at Heather. "But now that ye mention it, I would say she does. It's her little floppy ears, dinna ye think? And the impertinent tilt of her eyebrows. And her impish smile. But this gives me an idea. I've been wondering by what endearment I should call her. What do ye think of...my pixie?"

The old man beamed. "Och, laddie. It's perfect. I'm glad I thought of it for ye."

"Then so it shall be." Robbie exchanged a grin with Heather and scooped her in his arms to carry her over the threshold. "Welcome to Caithness...my pixie."

Also by Meara Platt

FARTHINGALE SERIES
My Fair Lily
The Duke I'm Going To Marry
Rules For Reforming A Rake
A Midsummer's Kiss
The Viscount's Rose
Earl Of Hearts
If You Wished For Me
Never Dare A Duke
Capturing The Heart Of A Cameron

BOOK OF LOVE SERIES
The Look of Love
The Touch of Love
The Taste of Love
The Song of Love
The Scent of Love
The Kiss of Love
The Chance of Love
The Gift of Love
The Heart of Love
The Hope of Love (novella)
The Dream of Love (novella)

DARK GARDENS SERIES
Garden of Shadows
Garden of Light

Garden of Dragons
Garden of Destiny
Garden of Angels

THE BRAYDENS
A Match Made In Duty
Earl of Westcliff
Fortune's Dragon
Earl of Kinross
Earl of Alnwick
Pearls of Fire★
(★also in Pirates of Britannia series)
Aislin
Gennalyn

DeWOLFE PACK ANGELS SERIES
Nobody's Angel
Kiss An Angel
Bhrodi's Angel

About the Author

Meara Platt is an award winning, USA TODAY bestselling author and an Amazon UK All-Star. Her favorite place in all the world is England's Lake District, which may not come as a surprise since many of her stories are set in that idyllic landscape, including her paranormal romance Dark Gardens series. Learn more about the Dark Gardens and Meara's lighthearted and humorous Regency romances in her Farthingale series and Book of Love series, or her warmhearted Regency romances in her Braydens series by visiting her website at www.mearaplatt.com.

Made in the USA
Coppell, TX
08 April 2022

76227263R00125